THE END IS NEAR

We have one more planet to visit before our journey is over. On Dargon, you will meet more creatures than ever before. Some tolerate each other. Others are at war. And you will need to convince all of them to help you retrieve the element. It will be no easy feat. Now is the time to band together and become a team . . . even with those we thought were enemies.

It has been a pleasure traveling with you, Voyagers. You have shown me more strength, creativity, and friendship than I could have imagined. I hope this is not good-bye forever. . . .

Chris,
Ship Specialist I Alpha Team

Elves and ogres at war.

Dragons of mass destruction.

And one last chance to save humankind.

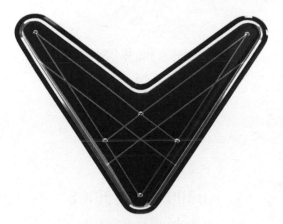

THE
SEVENTH ELEMENT

VOYAGERS

Don't miss a single Voyage. . . .

6
VOYAGERS

THE
SEVENTH ELEMENT

Wendy Mass

Random House 🏠 New York

Text copyright © 2016 by PC Studios Inc.
Full-color interior art, puzzles, and codes copyright © Animal Repair Shop
Voyagers digital and gaming experience by Animal Repair Shop

All rights reserved. Published in the United States by
Random House Children's Books,
a division of Penguin Random House LLC, New York.

Random House and the colophon are registered trademarks of
Penguin Random House LLC.

Visit us on the Web! randomhousekids.com

Educators and librarians, for a variety of teaching tools,
visit us at RHTeachersLibrarians.com

VoyagersHQ.com

Library of Congress Cataloging-in-Publication Data
is available upon request.
ISBN 978-0-385-38673-9 (trade) | ISBN 978-0-385-38675-3 (lib. bdg.) |
ISBN 978-0-385-38674-6 (ebook)

Printed in the United States of America
10 9 8 7 6 5 4 3 2 1
First Edition

Random House Children's Books supports the
First Amendment and celebrates the right to read.

For Chloe and Griffin—

I'd miss you if you went into space

to save the world.

1

On board the *Light Blade*'s transport ship, the *Clipper,* the Omega team began shouting at the same time as they strained against their seat straps.

"Where is she? Where's Piper?"

"Oh no!"

"How could we?"

Siena was the first to break down. Sobs racked her body. Tears flew out of her eyes.

Next to her, Niko began to rock back and forth in his chair, faster and faster. His mind sped back to the first day they'd all met. Piper had used her motorized wheelchair to pull him from the freezing water during their first competition at Base Ten. Then she had helped him recover from what should have been a fatal sting from the deadly Stingers on planet Infinity. That meant she'd saved his life *twice.* And he hadn't saved hers. Not once. Both he and Piper had trained to be medics, to help people. It no longer mattered that he had planned to tell Anna that holding Piper wasn't right. He should have *acted.*

With a gasp, Niko yanked himself free of his straps and began running up and down the length of the transport ship, a journey of about ten seconds. He knocked over the extra coats that Anna and Ravi hadn't used on their failed mission to planet Tundra, now a hundred miles below them. He pushed through swarms of ZRKs that had raced into the *Clipper* alongside the crew, and got a gash on his arm courtesy of one of the many nails that hadn't been fully hammered into the wall.

Niko knew Piper couldn't be hiding anywhere, but he had to look. The *Clipper* was tiny in comparison to the ship they'd just fled, but it would have easily accommodated all of them plus Piper. The *Clipper* could have fit *ten* Pipers, along with the air chair that had been specially made to allow her to travel in space. But there was no doubt—she was not on board.

He began tossing aside the crates that blocked the small back window. Maybe the *Light Blade* had a safety feature that would isolate a fire. It was possible, right? After all, their knowledge of the ship was on a need-to-know basis, and Colin—the alien clone in charge of the Omegas—rarely thought they needed to know anything.

Siena, Anna, and Ravi joined Niko. "Maybe the ZRKs were able to put out the flames," Ravi said, his voice tight with fear. "Those guys can do anything, right?"

But it only took one glance to see that the ZRKs—who did everything from cleaning up after them, to patching holes in the hull, to keeping the ship pressurized while traveling at Gamma Speed—must have had their limitations. They clearly couldn't stop the super-hot liquid metal the crew had taken from Meta

Prime from seeping through the floors and walls, igniting the oxygen that pumped through the vents. The Omega team members watched with sinking hearts as flames shot out from the back half of the ship, filling the sky with ash.

Colin was the only one facing the direction they were heading, rather than the direction they'd come from. He muttered and cursed as he piloted the ship toward the *Cloud Leopard*. All his careful planning, all their hard work, and they'd had to abandon their ship along with the elements they'd collected. The elements, when put together, would have created a source of power great enough to give him control over every living creature on Earth, or anywhere else he chose to take it. The safety of the little blond human was the least of his concerns. Now he'd have to figure out a way to wrestle the *Cloud Leopard* from the Alpha crew and from Chris, the brilliant alien he'd been cloned from and his arch-nemesis.

In the midst of his grumbling, Colin realized something. Maybe it wasn't such a bad thing that they were headed to the *Cloud Leopard*. He would have eventually had to go there to steal the zero crystals that his team had failed to retrieve from Tundra. And his team had also come up a few hundred Stinger spores short on Infinity. Once he had control, he would ditch the crew, turn the ship around, and go back to Aqua Gen to replace the Pollen Slither that was currently burning up back on the *Light Blade*. It was the only element so far that the Alpha team did not possess.

Colin leaned back in his seat to enjoy the last few minutes of the ride. Yes, this would work out just fine. Plus, the *Cloud Leopard* was a *much* nicer ship.

Anna heaved herself away from the window and ran up to the front. "Move!" she shouted at Colin. She tried to push his hand off the glass pad he was using to control the ship. Anna had made a lot of hard decisions on this trip—it was all part of being a leader—but this was an easy decision. No way they were leaving Piper behind.

Colin's hand didn't budge. His muscles were solid and unmovable, like a boulder. Anna realized she'd never actually touched him before. His skin felt cold. She yanked her hand back in surprise.

"Fine!" she snapped, flinging herself into her original seat. "I'll just take over from here." She slipped on the pair of flight glasses tucked into the armrest and prepared to wrest control of the ship. They were only a few thousand feet away from the docking bay of the *Cloud Leopard.* None of them had seen it up close before. If they hadn't been breathing heavily already, the sight of it would have taken their breath away.

"Stop!" Colin barked. "If you're trying to take us back to the *Light Blade,* that's a suicide mission!"

The others had joined them near the control panel.

"I don't care!" Anna focused all her might on getting the ship to turn around. It bucked and shook but didn't change course.

"Go, Anna!" Ravi exclaimed. He almost offered to take over, but Anna had mad flying skills and a look of determination on her face like he'd never seen. And he'd seen *lots* of determined looks on her face.

"Do it, Anna," Siena whispered, her heart pounding.

The *Clipper* swerved and bounced, finally slowing a tiny bit.

"Stop it!" Colin repeated.

But Anna only doubled her efforts. Her head pounded with the strain. She'd ridiculed the Alphas many times for not putting their individual needs first. Time and again she'd seen them risk their lives to help someone else, even if it meant losing a competition or even one of the precious elements they'd come so far for. Heck, they'd just saved her life down on Tundra after she'd been nothing but cruel to them this entire time. And arguably her cruelest act had been to kidnap Piper. She knew the girl was resourceful. No doubt Piper had been plotting a way to escape the training room. Maybe she'd found a place to hide that was still intact. If there was any chance of Anna redeeming herself by saving Piper, she had to try.

The *Clipper* suddenly soared upward, as if grabbed by an invisible wave, and then flung forward with such force that they nearly collided with the *Cloud Leopard*.

"Why did you do that?" Colin shouted, banking hard to the left to keep them from crashing into the hull of the massive ship.

"I didn't do anything!" Anna screamed back. "I'm trying to turn us around, remember?"

Ravi stretched out a shaking arm and pointed wordlessly out the back window.

They all looked out at what, in their current position, should have been the *Light Blade*. All that remained were pieces flying out in every direction.

The ship had exploded.

2

Team Alpha watched in horror from their navigation deck as the *Light Blade* exploded, sending chunks of the ship into the frozen white atmosphere of Tundra. Piper wasn't only their teammate; she was family. Carly fell back into her flight seat and began to sob. Gabriel sank into the next seat. He hugged his knees to his chest and buried his head.

"Chris!" Dash called across the room to where their resident alien was pounding on one of the keypads, trying to reach the *Light Blade* in case there was anything left to reach. Dash wiped at his eyes furiously. "Can you patch into the *Clipper*? Maybe Piper's with them after all."

Chris gave a nod, and a second later, they could hear the Omega crew shouting at each other. "Anna!" Dash screamed above the noise. "Do you have her? Did Piper make it on board with you?"

Instantly, the voices stopped. Dash thought they'd lost the connection. Then: "I'm so sorry, Dash," Anna said. "I wanted to go back, but—"

"Turn it off," Dash ordered. Chris complied. "STEAM," Dash said, "what are the odds of surviving that blast? Maybe it looked worse than it was?"

STEAM did not hesitate. "I do not think you want the odds, sir. No sir."

Dash sank into the seat next to the hunched-over Gabriel. Piper was so strong and brave and kind, and they were finally about to get her back. Why was time always their enemy? He felt something inside himself begin to break. He couldn't handle this.

No one spoke. No one knew how to comfort anyone else.

Through the sound of Carly's sobs, Gabriel's brain half registered a vibration through his Mobile Tech Band. He ignored it. Probably an alarm telling him it was time to exercise more. He didn't want to exercise. He didn't want to do anything. He never wanted to move from that chair.

Then he heard a ding. Then another ding. As his finger moved to turn the sound off, his eyes flitted over the screen out of habit. He sat bolt upright. "Guys! Guys! Look at this!"

No one moved. He reached out and shook Carly and Dash until they focused on him. Then he held up his arm so they could all read the words on the screen.

Opn th pid bat doos, hak.

Dash looked at Gabriel like he was crazy, then turned away. Carly could barely see the screen through her tears. Why was Gabriel showing them some garbled old message? How could he even care about anything other than Piper right now? Carly, too, turned away.

But Gabriel jumped to his feet, heart pounding. He shouted into his communicator, "Hello? Hello?"

Another ding.

Sorry, hrd to typ in space suit.
SUMI translating to speech hang on.

A second later, a high-pitched voice echoed through the navigation deck. It said only one sentence: "Open the pod bay doors, Hal."

Gabriel burst out laughing and crying at the same time. Leave it to Piper to use the famous line from science-fiction film history. The others looked at him with shocked expressions. They still didn't understand. How could they? No one knew he'd hacked into SUMI's system (which was a lot like STEAM's) in order to communicate with Piper on the *Light Blade*. And now the robot was telling him she was alive! Not only alive, but outside the ship right at that moment!

"Piper needs us to open the docking bay doors!" he shouted. "She's outside!"

Chris ran to his station and quickly activated the doors. Dash grabbed Gabriel's arm. "Do you mean it? It's really possible?" His eyes were so wide Gabriel thought they might bulge out of his face. Chris and Carly gathered around for Gabriel's answer. Carly held her breath, not ready to let herself get excited. STEAM spun in circles repeating, "Open the pod bay doors, Hal, open the pod bay doors, Hal." Behind him, TULIP turned in circles too.

Gabriel filled them in on what he'd done while they were down on Tundra. "She must have figured out a way to power her chair and took off before the explosion!"

In quick succession, they all launched themselves into the tubes that connected most of the rooms on the ship. This was one time no one wanted to compete for the longest route. They arrived in the engine room just in time to see the cargo bay doors close behind Piper's air chair. They ran onto the loading dock and surrounded her, all leaping and crying and grabbing at her. SUMI got some of this affection too, since she was sitting sideways on Piper's lap.

Chris undid the straps holding them in, lifted SUMI off, and plopped the shiny black robot down next to Piper's chair. SUMI nodded her oversized head at them and chirped happily. "Quite a ride," she said with a giggle. "Quite a ride!"

Carly rushed toward Piper, with Dash right on her heels.

Piper pulled off her round helmet and beamed at them. "Miss me?"

"More than you can imagine," Dash replied as he scooped her out of the chair. Even with the added weight of Piper's space suit, it felt like carrying air. He ran in circles with her while Carly and Gabriel laughed.

"Put me back," Piper commanded, but she was laughing too. Normally she'd never let anyone carry her, but right now, somehow, she didn't mind.

Dash gently placed her back in her chair, noting it had gotten pretty banged up. Good thing they had spares. "How did you escape?" he asked. He checked around the back of the air chair. "I don't see the rocket canisters we sent you with."

"I couldn't get to them, but I found another way." Piper gestured at SUMI. "Show them," she said.

SUMI giggled and hopped up and down on her springy legs

until her back was facing the group. Then she unhinged a flap over her rear end, and a puff of steam blew out.

After a few seconds of stunned silence, the Alpha crew—including STEAM and Chris—roared with laughter.

Piper wiped her eyes and said, "It was a surprise to me too. And I've spent a lot of time with her these past few weeks."

"Her?" STEAM asked.

Piper grinned. "It's not like we paint our toenails together or anything. But, yeah, I think of her as a girl."

"I think STEAM's jealous," Carly declared. "He's used to being the only robot on board."

TULIP made a disapproving clicking sound, and Carly bent down to rub the tiny robot's warm belly. "Sorry, TULIP."

STEAM's blue lights flickered on and off, and he hovered away in a huff. SUMI hopped after him.

"Looks like the start of a beautiful friendship," Gabriel said with a grin.

Piper reached over and gave his arm a squeeze. "Thank you," she said. "If you hadn't hacked into SUMI, I wouldn't have thought to go back to the training room for her. We both would have gone down with the *Light Blade*. Or if I managed to power over here some other way, I wouldn't have been able to let you know I was outside. You totally saved me."

Gabriel blushed. Then he frowned. "I should have done something sooner."

"There was nothing you could do while we were in Gamma Speed," she said. "I know that. I shouldn't have been so trusting of Colin and Anna in the first place. I should have insisted on proof."

"C'mon, Piper," Carly said, swooping in, "let's go back to our room. It's been way too quiet in there without you."

"Sounds good," said Piper, giving Gabriel's arm one more squeeze. "I can't wait for my comfortable bed."

"We should probably check in with the *Clipper*," Dash said reluctantly. Chris nodded.

"I'll tell you all about our adventure on Tundra as a bedtime story," Carly said as she and Piper started across the room. Piper stopped short, spinning her air chair back around. "That's right! In all the excitement, I actually forgot the point of the mission! Did you guys get the zero crystals?"

"You better believe it, sister!" Carly said, holding out her fist to Piper.

"That's great!" Piper said, returning Carly's fist bump. "I don't think Omega's got them. They came back in a really bad mood. A worse mood than usual, that is."

Carly and Dash exchanged a surprised look. "Are you sure?" Dash asked.

Piper nodded, then coughed. "Be right back." She floated across the room to one of the water stations that the ZRKs kept stocked with cold water. Traveling through space with only a butt-propulsion robot made a girl thirsty!

Back on the dock, Gabriel whooped. "That means we beat them. They can't get all six elements now! And we . . . we . . ." He trailed off as the realization hit him. The *Light Blade* had exploded. He sank down to the floor. "We can't either!"

3

Dash and Carly were only realizing it now. The Pollen Slither—the only element they'd failed to retrieve, the only element Team Omega had gotten instead of them—had been on the *Light Blade*. Blood drained from their faces. All the adrenaline that had kept Dash from crashing seemed to seep from his body. Not only had the mission failed, but he would have no way to get home. None of them would have a way to get home at all. Utterly defeated, he slunk to the floor beside Gabriel. Carly joined them. They sat in a circle, heads bowed. Nobody said anything. What was there to say? They'd let everyone down. The entire human race.

Piper made her way back over to the group. "Whatcha doing?" she asked, curious. "Aren't you guys a little old for Duck, Duck, Goose?" Or maybe they'd made up some new game in her absence. A lot can change in a few weeks.

Chris tentatively reached out his hand and laid it on top of Piper's. She was surprised at the warmth of it. "The mission is over," he said, trying to put as much emotion into his voice as he could. He knew the others thought him devoid of it, but it wasn't true. "We cannot make the Source," he told her, "without the Pollen Slither. It could not have survived the blast."

Piper looked down at her three friends hunched over in their circle, and then up at Chris as his words sunk in. Her eyes widened.

"You're right! It couldn't have survived the blast," she said seriously. Then she twisted around in her chair and flipped open a storage space behind her headrest. "Good thing it wasn't on the ship when it exploded. I took it from the engine room before I left." She held up her hand to reveal an iridescent liquid inside of what looked like an ordinary mayonnaise jar.

For the first time in his very long life, Chris felt like weeping as he hugged her and her chair at the same time. Carly and Gabriel jumped up so fast they bonked heads. Piper couldn't tell if they were laughing or crying, and settled on a combination of both. Dash was a bit slower to his feet, but his joy at her news soon gave him enough energy to join the others as they jumped up and down.

Chris beamed at all of them. "No doubt about it. Shawn Phillips picked the four best candidates in the entire world for this mission."

"No more surprises," Dash ordered the crew, raking his fingers through his hair. "I honestly can't take it."

As if the Omegas had heard his words, they chose that moment to chime in through the intercom system. "Request permission to board," Anna said. She sounded weary. Dash really,

really did not want to deal with her—or Colin. Especially Colin. Dash grimaced and closed his eyes.

"What took them so long?" Carly asked Chris.

"The shock wave likely knocked out their engines," Chris explained. "They probably had to drift here."

Piper handed the jar of Pollen Slither to Chris and turned her air chair away from the docking bay. "If you don't mind, I'm going to sit this reunion out."

"Yeah, me too," Carly said. The two girls hurried from the room.

Gabriel nudged Dash and gestured toward the docking bay. "Guess you should answer them."

"Guess so," Dash replied, but he didn't move toward the communication system.

"They'll need to know about Piper too," Gabriel added. The Omegas had treated them all so poorly—both on the planets and in outer space—that a small part of him wanted to hold off telling them Piper was safe, just so they'd feel bad a little longer. He glanced at Dash and wondered if he was thinking the same thing.

Then Gabriel sighed. He had liked them all back on Base Ten. He'd even grudgingly admired Anna's drive to win all the time. They were dealing with that weird alien clone. He'd like to think he would have behaved better in their shoes, but who knows? He still regretted being kind of snappy with Dash those first few weeks in space.

He was about to nudge Dash again, when the Alpha team leader took a deep breath and squared up his shoulders. Gabriel couldn't help noticing that all the excitement of the day had taken its toll on Dash. His skin looked a little gray. Gabriel sure wasn't going to point that out, though.

"All right," Dash announced. "Here goes. Chris, can you open the docking bay doors? Tell them they can park beside the *Cloud Cat.* Give them the good news about Piper and escort them all to the training room. They can buckle into the flight simulation seats to prepare for the jump to Gamma Speed."

Chris nodded and strode to the other end of the engine room to ready the docking bay. Dash spoke into his Mobile Tech Band. "Alphas, meet on the flight deck to prepare for Gamma Speed. Piper, I'm sorry you won't have time to rest. We need to make up for lost time."

Dash hoped that last part didn't sound too selfish; he hadn't meant it that way. But for all the good news that day, he wasn't getting any younger. He'd rest when they went into Gamma.

Right after he figured out what to do with their "guests."

4

From the control panel on the arm of his flight seat, Dash switched on the large monitor above their heads that allowed them to see into most of the rooms on board. He pulled up the view of the training center. He wasn't ready to see the Omega team's faces yet, but he knew he had to do his duty as captain. He took a deep breath and forced himself to look at the screen.

The Omega team were already strapped into the simulation seats. "Prepare for Gamma—" he began. His voice cracked on the last word. They looked so miserable! Anna's face was as swollen as a boxer after losing a big fight. The other three looked pale and sweaty. His anger at them faded fast. He hadn't considered they might be upset about losing their ship, but of course they had to be. He'd be devastated if the *Cloud Leopard* went up in smoke.

He cleared his throat. They all looked up, clearly just noticing that the screen in front of them had been turned on. "I'm very sorry about your ship," Dash said, meaning it. "I'm sure the *Light Blade* was a great—"

"How can you even *think* about that?" Anna shouted up at the screen. "We're the ones who are sorry. It's because of us—*me* really—that Piper's gone. And the Pollen Slither! How will we get home now if we can't make the Source?" She said this last part as if just realizing it for the first time. Then she cried even harder. "This is all my fault! I'll never forgive myself. Never. I don't care if you believe me or not."

Dash's eyes opened wide. He twisted around in his seat to face Chris. "Didn't you tell them?"

Chris shook his head. "There was no time. I had to ready the ship. You may have forgotten our time predicament, but I have not."

Dash opened his mouth to argue, but what was the point? Chris probably wasn't trying to be cruel by withholding the news of Piper's return. For all Chris's decades on Earth, he still hadn't quite picked up on appropriate social behavior.

Dash turned back to the view screen and moved the controls to widen the angle. Now the entire navigation deck would be visible to the Omegas. All at once, they strained against their straps, gasping with wide eyes.

Siena spoke first. Relief flooded over her usually guarded face. "Piper! Is that you? Is it really you?"

Piper waved at the screen. "Hi, guys. Yes, it's me."

Ravi spoke next. "You're not some crazy hologram, just trying to mess with us?"

Piper smiled. "That'd be cool, but no."

Anna and Niko stopped gaping long enough for Anna to stutter, "But . . . but . . . how?"

Piper shrugged. "The same way I got to your ship in the first place." She glanced at the others beside her and winked. "Well, mostly the same."

Next to her, Carly giggled.

Dash spoke up. "Chris was supposed to tell you when you arrived, but there was a . . ." He glanced at the alien currently gesturing madly toward the Gamma Speed button. "A miscommunication," Dash finished. "Once we're safely in Gamma, we'll explain about Piper and the plans for the rest of the mission."

"You mean *our* mission," Niko said, speaking up for the first time. "We're helping now." Then he waved, almost shyly, at Piper. "Hi, Piper. Thank you for being alive." He bowed his head at her. She saluted.

Dash noticed the look of determination on each of the Omegas' faces. In a way, Niko was right—the Alphas were going to need every advantage they could get on the next planet, and these four did have major skills. He wouldn't turn down help from anyone. Well, maybe from Colin. Speaking of . . .

"Chris! Where's Colin? Wasn't he on the *Clipper*?"

"He is being held in my private quarters," Chris replied. "We will discuss it later. Gamma Speed in five . . . four . . ."

Three seconds later, everyone gripped the arms of their seats as their bodies pressed deeper into the backs of the chairs. Gabriel had once said that going into Gamma felt like an invisible hand pushing on his chest. But soon the pressure released, and the burning embers of the *Light Blade* were hundreds of light-years away.

The Alphas began unstrapping themselves. "We need to go talk to them," Dash said.

Down in the training room, none of the Omegas moved. They wore matching puzzled expressions. "Didn't he say we were going into Gamma Speed?" Ravi asked Anna.

She looked around at the room, which, after the mild shaking, seemed completely unchanged. Nothing looked warped, or stretchy, and she didn't feel the slightest bit nauseous or dizzy. She nodded grimly and could barely keep the hysteria out of her voice. "This ship is broken. We're all trapped in space."

Siena groaned. "We were finally going to be a team!"

Anna raised an eyebrow. "What do you mean *finally*?"

Siena and Niko exchanged glances. They both knew they never should have stood by while Anna held Piper hostage on board the *Light Blade*. Anna had said they needed "insurance" that the Alpha crew wouldn't leave them stranded in deep space. But Niko and Siena knew that the Alpha team would never have left anyway. Instead, they had let their fear of Anna's temper keep them just as much a prisoner as Piper.

Niko sat up straighter. "Yes, Anna, *finally*. Siena and I have had it with the way you treat everyone, never letting any of us share an opinion or make our own decisions. We've always wanted out, but now it doesn't matter. Without Gamma Speed, we'll never, ever make it back to Earth."

Anna opened her mouth, closed it, and opened it again. The others just didn't understand that being the leader required making the toughest choices, taking the biggest risks. Hadn't she always kept her crew safe? Well, mostly safe? They had beaten the Alpha team nearly every time because of her. But then, when she thought Piper was dead, and it was her fault, something had snapped inside her. She'd gone too far. And why? To impress someone millions of miles away with how clever she could be? She was *done* doing things based on what others thought of her. She was *done* trying to impress anyone.

So she pursed her lips and crossed her arms and didn't say anything. The other three sat there and pouted right along with her.

The door to the training center slid open. Dash walked in, followed by Carly and Gabriel, with Piper pulling up the rear in a new air chair.

"Why are you guys still strapped into your seats?" Gabriel asked. "The next sixty-one days in Gamma are gonna pass *really* slowly that way."

"But how are we in Gamma?" Niko asked. He unbuckled quickly and jumped up. The others followed, a bit more hesitantly. Niko rested a hand against the smooth white wall. "It doesn't even feel like we're moving."

"You've been following our Gamma stream across the universe for over nine months now," Gabriel pointed out. "You know what Gamma Speed feels like."

No one replied until Ravi burst out laughing. "This is what it's like for them!" The rest of the Omega team paused, then broke into cheers and laughter themselves.

"It was really bad over there," Piper explained to the Alphas.

"Being in Gamma Speed felt like your body was being stretched in ten different directions. And it lasts pretty much the whole time."

"Really? Wow," Carly said, feeling a flicker of pity. Now that they were up close and not running from each other on an alien world, she could see how the Omega crew had aged since they'd all hung out at the base over a year ago. She supposed she didn't look like a little kid anymore either.

"That bites," Gabriel agreed. "Bet you're glad you're here now."

At the same time, Siena and Niko said, "You have no idea."

"Totally," Ravi said. Then to Anna, he added, "No offense."

"Yeah right." She grunted and kicked the nearest chair, but a hint of a smile flitted across her face. Anna might not miss the old ship too much, but Dash had no doubt she'd miss being in charge. He would have to move slowly with her if they were going to function as one big team. And that was a big *if.*

"C'mon," Dash said, beckoning them to follow him out of the training room. "It's been a long day for everyone. Quick tour so you know the lay of the land; then we'll eat and sleep. Chris has called a meeting in the morning to figure everything out."

Carly stepped in as tour guide. She pointed out the different rooms as they passed, and explained how the transport tubes that crisscrossed the ship worked. She left out the part about the contest to see who could take the longest route. She wanted to keep that as something the four Alphas did.

"We had those tubes on the *Light Blade,*" Ravi said. "But they only went directly from one level to the other. No twisty stuff in the middle just for kicks. Colin didn't put anything on the *Light Blade* just for kicks." As they passed the relaxation room, Ravi caught sight of the video game screens built into the walls and tabletops. His eyes opened wide at the virtual reality station. "You've got to be *kidding* me!" That started the Omegas pointing out all the things that were better on the *Cloud Leopard*. Dash had to admit he felt proud of his ship. He tried not to dwell on the fact that it would fall apart if Chris's old, tiny beaten-up ship hidden beneath the engine room decided to fail. Other than Chris, Dash was still the only one on board who knew about it, and he planned to keep it that way. The crew had enough to worry about.

When the tour reached the sleeping quarters, the four newcomers instantly quieted. Both doors had slid open at the same time, and the Omegas looked from the boys' dorm to the girls', their eyes wide. Then Niko and Ravi ran into the boys' bedroom, while Anna and Siena ran into the girls'.

Siena gave a small cry. Piper gasped and pulled up short in her chair.

"What's wrong?" Carly asked, stepping inside the room. She blinked twice. *Huh?* She and Piper had just been in this room not even an hour ago. But it looked very different now. Somehow, it had grown to twice the size! The room was both taller and wider, and easily accommodated the additional bunk bed that now sat a few feet away from theirs. The walls displayed pictures not only of Carly's and Piper's families, but of Anna's and Siena's now too, along with maps of all their hometowns. The walls sparkled with a fresh coat of yellow paint, and a super-thick white carpet

replaced the pink one that Carly had always thought was too girly. The ZRKs had been *very* busy!

"Wow," Anna said with a low whistle. "This is almost as nice as the room I won back at Base Ten!"

Across the hall, Ravi flung himself to the floor and ran his arms back and forth along the plush carpet. Niko joined him, and after a moment's hesitation, Gabriel followed.

"Dude," Gabriel said, twisting his head to look up at Dash. "You've gotta try this."

Dash laughed and shook his head. "Someone's gotta run this ship."

"I agree," Anna's voice said from behind him. "You offering me a job?"

Dash jumped back, startled. He'd have to work on getting used to having her so close. "Hardly," he said dryly. "Surely you notice that every time I suggest we work as a team, you double-cross me? Starting with that holo Raptagon back at the base. And then basically every other time I've seen you."

She shrugged. "Okay, I get it. Teamwork's not my thing. I'll try harder, I promise."

Dash narrowed his eyes at her. "And I should trust you because . . . ?"

She looked him in the eye and whispered, "Because I know your secret."

5

"**Chris, you have** outdone yourself tonight, my man," Gabriel said as he sat down next to Carly at the dinner table. He rubbed his hands together in anticipation of the tasty meal.

Chris nodded his head at the compliment. He knew it had been a very long and difficult day for both crews and wanted to do something nice for them. Plus, preparing the food got him into the kitchen and away from Colin, who gave him the creeps. Looking at him was like looking in a fun-house mirror, but without the fun. The clone was currently fuming, trapped as he was by the newly created force field that would keep everyone out of Chris's private quarters—and keep Colin in. At least until Chris could determine if Colin was a threat to the success of the mission.

Niko, Ravi, and Siena stared at the dinner set out before them. Steaming plates of meats, vegetables, and pies, refreshing piles of cut fruit, chocolates, cookies, ice cream, and lemonade covered the long table. Ravi actually began to drool. "You eat like this every night?" he asked. On the *Light Blade*, if it wasn't freeze-dried, powdered, or pressed into the shape of a bar, they didn't carry it.

Carly grinned. "Yup! Every meal. Don't you?"

Piper elbowed her good-naturedly. "Don't listen to her. Chris only cooks for us on special nights—like right before a mission or when we come back. The ZRKs just feed us whatever's been programmed into the system. It's usually pretty good, though," she admitted.

"Where are Dash and Anna?" Carly asked, glancing at the door to the dining hall. The rest of them were all there.

"Dunno," Gabriel replied, already piling his plate high with food. "Probably talking about captain stuff, you know, who's going to do what now that we're all on one ship."

Carly and Siena shared a look across the table. As second-in-command on their respective ships, they both felt a pang of jealousy. They were used to being in on their captain's plans. Well, Carly more than Siena. And now with two captains, where would that leave them?

"Shouldn't we wait for them?" Piper asked. "You know, to be polite?"

The three boys all had forks heading toward their mouths.

"Oh, never mind," Piper said, reaching for her favorite—a peanut-butter-and-Nutella cookie. "You snooze, you lose."

"If you won't tell me what you know about me, then tell me this—why did you guys really take Piper?" Dash demanded. "You knew we wouldn't leave you behind. We'd proven that each time. And then when you got the Pollen Slither and we didn't, you had your 'insurance' right there. So why do it?"

Anna knew he'd eventually ask her point-blank. She could blame it on Ike Phillips, and Dash would probably believe it. But lies had a way of coming undone, and she didn't want to risk it. She had no desire to be stuck on the sidelines while the Alpha team completed their mission. She took a deep breath. "Making sure you guys didn't get the Pollen Slither was Ike's idea. He wanted to make sure you needed us. I guess I wanted to one-up him. To come up with something even bigger and bolder."

Dash didn't say anything. Anna felt her cheeks grow hot. Saying it out loud made it sound pretty bad. She cleared her throat. "The others didn't know about it. I knew they wouldn't want to, so I didn't give them a choice."

"And you're surprised they wanted to leave?"

Anna shrugged. "My father always said that successful leaders don't have friends; they have employees."

"You talk a lot about your dad and his opinions."

Anna crossed her arms. "Don't you listen to *your* father? I'll bet he—"

"My dad is gone," Dash said, his jaw hardening. "I don't know how he'd feel about leadership or success or anything, really."

"Oh," Anna said, taken aback. "Sorry."

Dash could see in her eyes that she meant it. He softened. "Look, it's over now. Piper's back, and we have a chance to make a new beginning, as one big team. If there's something you know about me, just say it. If we're going to work together, we have to be open and honest with each other."

"Is that what you've been doing?" she asked. "Being honest with your crew? Do they even know?"

"Do they even know *what*?" He was pretty sure he knew what secret she'd been referring to, but how did she know? He had planned to tell the Omega team about his situation but had hoped to do it later on in the trip so they didn't question his ability to lead the team.

Anna sighed dramatically. She could keep him guessing, but the smells drifting in from the dining hall next door were really amazing and she was starving. "Fine," she snapped. "Does your crew even know that you have approximately sixty-five days left to live?"

27

Dash cringed. "Do you have to put it quite so . . . bluntly?"

"How else should I put it?" she replied.

"Yes, they know," he said. "Admittedly I didn't tell them for a long time because I didn't want to worry them or make them think anything was wrong with me. But now . . ." He trailed off.

She assessed him carefully. Not much got past her. They all looked exhausted, but Dash had deeper circles under his eyes, almost like hollows. And his light brown hair— usually so full and wavy—was matted to his head. She finished his sentence. "But now you're starting to show signs. You're breaking down."

"I guess I am," he admitted. "It's not too bad, just a tiredness that sweeps over me sometimes. I take shots every day that keep me healthy, but as it gets closer to the deadline, they've started to be less effective. Anyway, how did you know about this? Did you eavesdrop when Commander Phillips told me about it?"

She shook her head. "Nope. I knew you guys had some private talks, but I put the puzzle pieces together myself. When we first got to the base and I finally met my competitors, I looked everyone up on the Internet. Knowledge is power, you know. I saw everyone's birthdays but didn't think anything of it. One day, Colin mentioned Chris had developed some kind of serum that allowed older people to survive Gamma Speed. Then I remembered what the commander had said about why they needed kids our exact age, and I remembered your birth date. I'm smart that way, remember?"

Dash rubbed his eyes. So tired. "You're smart in a lot of ways, Anna," he said wearily. "I just wish you'd use your brain for good, instead of . . . well, the opposite. If we're going to work together—and I hope we are—then no more games."

Anna put out her hand. "No more games," she said.

Dash hesitated. Could he really trust her, after everything she'd done? But Chris had told Dash that he wasn't going to have enough strength to go on this last mission. What if Anna had to replace him as the leader? He was going to need someone who could make tough decisions. And Anna had a history of making some really tough decisions. . . .

Dash finally took Anna's hand and shook it firmly. "Okay, then," he said. "Now let's go see if they left us any food. Piper's been known to eat all the cookies if you don't get there fast enough."

Anna's eyes brightened. "You have *cookies*?"

Dash grinned. "Race you?"

"I don't know," Anna said. "In your present weakened condition, it might not be a fair fight."

But Dash was already gone. Anna smiled. For the first time that she could remember, she would let someone else win.

6

Everyone sat around the long table in the training room the next morning, waiting for Chris. Dash checked the time. "He's usually very prompt," he assured the new crew members. Having a meeting like this was unusual for the Alpha team. Unless there was a lot of specialized training necessary, Chris usually didn't bother to brief them about their next mission until they were much closer to their destination. The earliness of this meeting was making everyone feel a little on edge.

While they waited, Niko asked Piper to show him the medical bay after the meeting. Dash knew it would be fun for her to compare notes with someone. Ravi and Gabriel had a total nerdfest talking old video games, new high-tech stuff on the ship, fantasy novels, and how they would beat the other in chess and Pac-Man. Siena sat quietly. Dash could tell she was churning something over in her mind. Only one scowl and a grunt had passed between Anna and Carly. He decided that was progress.

In fact, it almost felt like old times. Back at Base Ten, they'd shared a feeling of camaraderie. And at dinner last night, Dash could sense that feeling start to return. They still couldn't help exchanging stories and joking. On a serious note, Niko had admitted that he only got through the nine months on the *Light Blade* by meditating whenever he was alone. This time no one made fun of him. Dash asked him if he'd show them how to do it, and he'd agreed. But all Dash heard before he fell asleep was Niko instructing, "Now close your eyes and relax your body." Dash looked forward to catching more of the lesson that night.

Finally, Chris hurried into the room. "Thank you for waiting. I'm sorry I'm late."

"Let me guess," Gabriel said. "Dealing with your evil alien clone took longer than you expected?"

Chris looked surprised, which for him was a big deal since he didn't often show emotion. "Yes!" he said. "Colin is proving to be quite difficult."

"He thinks he should run the ship, right?" Anna asked. "It must be killing him to be kept in one room like that, away from all the action."

"Yeah," Piper said. "That must be the worst."

Anna turned to face her. "Hey, I said I was sorry."

"Did you really?" Piper asked. "I don't seem to recall that."

The two stared at each other until Anna said, "Well if I didn't, I'm saying it now."

When Anna didn't say anything else, Piper asked, "That was it?"

Anna gave a groan. "I'm sorry! I'm sorry times ten. Is that good enough?"

Piper grinned. "It's okay. You actually did me a favor."

"Huh?" Anna (and everyone else) said.

Piper nodded. "Yup. I was lying in bed last night thinking how happy I was to be back on the ship, with my team and Chris and STEAM and Rocket." She paused to bend over and scratch the dog behind his ears. He hadn't left her side since her return.

She continued. "And suddenly I realized something. I was the right person to go over there. Niko was seriously ill from being hit by the Stinger spore, and my training and his instincts helped cure him."

Dash looked at Niko in surprise. He hadn't known he'd been hit by a spore. Wasn't that supposed to be fatal?

Then Piper said, "And anyone else—anyone whose legs actually worked—wouldn't have been able to fly up to the ceiling to discover the slogger was leaking. The crew wouldn't have had those few minutes of warning. And when they forgot me, I was the only one who could have traveled through outer space without a spaceship." Piper leaned back in her chair. "I was meant to be there. Maybe I should be thanking you for the opportunity to help."

Anna opened her mouth. Carly pointed a finger at her. "Don't you dare say *you're welcome.*"

"Who, me?" Anna said innocently.

Siena leaned across the table to Piper. "Will you ever forgive me for yesterday? Those last few minutes were so crazy and everyone was running and Colin was shouting at us and there was no room for thought. I know it's no excuse," she said, not even waiting for Piper's response. "But it's like Colin and Ike

Phillips brainwashed us or something, convincing us you guys would fail, and it would be up to us to save the world at any cost. I got mixed up."

"We all did," Ravi said firmly. "But now we're exactly where we're supposed to be. And we're going to make up for all the things we did wrong. Whatever we can do to help for the rest of the mission, you can count on us."

"That's good," Chris said, wearing a very serious expression. "Because there will be no room for competition on planet Dargon. Before we went into Gamma Speed yesterday, I was able to get a quick message to the base. We will be too far from Earth to send or receive messages for the rest of the voyage. I will work on strengthening the signal, but I wouldn't count on it. I had only a minute to brief Shawn—Commander Phillips, that is —on our current situation. At first, he was concerned that you were here under false pretenses. That you were trying to sabotage the mission for us."

The Omega team began to protest. Chris raised his hand. "He trusts you, don't worry. It's his father he doesn't trust. I assured him you all had the best of intentions to help. He always felt bad that he wasn't able to send all eight of you originally, so he was happy that you would be working together. As we get closer to our destination, I will brief you on what will be expected of you and how to prepare. Until then, I need you all to work on becoming one team."

Hearing this, Dash put his hand in the middle of the table. After a beat, Carly laid hers on top. Then Siena, followed by Niko, Gabriel, and Ravi. Piper floated up in her chair so that she could lean over and place hers on top of Ravi's. They all looked at Anna. She lifted her hand, then glanced up at Piper as if to ask for permission. Piper gave a small nod. Anna rested her hand on top of Piper's.

Dash tried to think of something "leaderlike" to say. He almost repeated what Shawn had often told them at base—*failure is not an option.* But that made his stomach twist a little when he heard it. It was too much pressure. So instead, he just said, "All in."

"All in," the others repeated.

"Good," Chris said, nodding his satisfaction as they pulled their hands away. "I will have new uniforms delivered to your rooms this afternoon. I trust you to know how you will best serve this ship and this mission. Conserve your strength. This will be our hardest retrieval yet against your toughest foes."

"Don't worry," Gabriel told the others with a wink. "He says that each time."

"I do not," Chris said, unaware he was being teased.

"I'm pretty sure it can't be harder than pulling a tooth out of a dinosaur the size of a building," Piper said.

Dash nodded. "Or dodging fireballs of molten lava in some crazy steampunk city."

"Or dodging pirates and Thermites and Predator Zs!" Carly added.

"Or Stinger spores and murderous Saws," Siena said with a shudder.

Gabriel grinned. "You guys notice we do an awful lot of dodging?"

Everyone laughed except Chris. He still wore his serious expression. "I admit, all those missions were challenging. But now, in order to have any chance of retrieving the element, you'll have to convince three different kinds of species to work with you. And trust me, that won't be easy."

After a few seconds of silence, Ravi said, "They're werewolves, aren't they?"

"They are not werewolves," Chris said.

Ravi pretended to look disappointed.

"I bet it's ghosts!" Siena said.

"Giant marshmallow men!" Gabriel shouted.

"Come on, guys," Anna said firmly. "Let Chris talk."

"Thank you, Anna," Chris said. But before he could say anything else, Anna said, "It's vampires, isn't it? Blood-sucking vampires?"

They all laughed again. Anna grinned.

Chris laid his head on the table. "So this is what having eight kids on board one spaceship is going to be like."

"Teenagers," Carly corrected him. "We're all thirteen now."

Before someone could point out that they'd celebrated everyone's thirteenth birthday during their voyage except his, Dash quickly jumped in. "Sorry, Chris. We'll try to be more mature. Won't we, guys?"

Everyone grumbled good-naturedly, but agreed. "So what's so bad on this planet?" Dash asked.

"Well, you need to gather fresh dragon cinder. That is going to require working with the various life-forms of the planet. First there are the elves, whose trust you will need to gain right away."

"Elves?" Ravi repeated. "Like the gentle woodland creatures with pointy ears?"

"Yes," Chris answered. "You will need them as allies. Fortunately, their language is not that different from your own, so communicating with them won't require the use of your translator."

"That sounds like a cakewalk," Ravi said. "What else ya got?"

"Ogres," Chris said.

"Sweet!"

Everyone turned to look at Gabriel as though he'd lost his mind.

"What?" he said with a shrug. "That Shrek guy is cool, right?"

"Actually," Chris said, "ogres are terrible creatures. They attack the peaceful elves on a whim and will do anything to hoard as much silver and other metal as they can. They are cruel, angry, and spiteful."

"They sound lovely," Piper said. "Let's steer clear of them, shall we?"

Chris shook his head. "Unfortunately, you will need them. They're the only ones who can lead you to the dragons."

Niko sat up straight. "Dude! Did you say *dragons*?"

Chris nodded. "That is the third and by far the fiercest creature you will encounter."

"Awesome!" Niko replied, giving a high five to Gabriel and Ravi. "You were right, Siena!"

Chris looked puzzled. "Siena, you knew there'd be dragons?"

Siena nodded. "It's a gift I have, seeing the future."

"Interesting," Chris said, typing into his Mobile Tech Band. "That wasn't in your profile material. I'm going to have to speak to Shawn about being more thorough. Anyone else have a surprise talent they've kept hidden?"

Piper glanced at Niko. When she was helping him recover from the Stinger poison, something extraordinary had happened. Niko's health had turned around overnight, but she couldn't quite attribute his rapid recovery to the medicine she'd cooked up.

"I'm kidding," Siena told Chris. "Of course I can't see the future. Niko has a thing for dragons, and we were talking about it one day, that's all."

"Oh," Chris said, clearly disappointed. He reached back over to his MTB and hit the delete key.

Niko saw Piper looking at him, and quickly looked down at the table. Piper shook her head. She'd learned that Niko was too modest about his gift—the way he'd been able to speed his own recovery through acupressure was truly amazing. It was like his hands were filled with magic!

"Anything else we should know now about the mission?" Dash asked. He knew he wasn't going—he couldn't risk that his worsening condition would put the others at risk. It was a big blow, but what choice did he have? He was trying to focus on their journey right now, not their destination. There would be plenty of time for that. Before Chris could answer, Dash added, "I'd really like to get everyone started with their new jobs on the ship."

Chris hesitated before answering. There was more he could tell them about his history with the elves. He looked around the table and noticed the anxious faces staring back at him. He sighed. Why steal their last moments of relative safety? Let them have fun while they're in this last period of Gamma Speed. Without the

Source, it wasn't only Dash who wouldn't live to see home again. It was all of them.

So Chris shook his head. "I'm done for now." The kids jumped up, like it was the end of the day at school and they were sprung. "One more thing," he said, ignoring the few groans he heard. "Here." He handed a Mobile Tech Band to each of the Omegas. "We made extras for the Alpha team in case one was damaged on a mission. Now you should have them."

He showed them how to slip them on and adjust them to the size of their forearm. "Totally cool," Niko said, already programming it to monitor his pulse and heart rate. "Thanks!"

"We had something like this," Anna said. "A little smaller and not as comfortable. But Colin never let us wear them unless we were on a mission. I think he didn't want us to be able to communicate with each other behind his back."

Dash stood back and watched everyone playing with their MTBs. Chris joined him. "Time for your injection," he said quietly.

Dash glanced at the group. The members of the Alpha team were showing the Omegas some of the cooler things the MTB could do. He'd have to stop thinking of them as Alphas and Omegas now that they were one team. They needed a new name.

No one noticed Dash and Chris slip out of the room. Rocket followed at their heels as they headed toward Chris's quarters.

"Did you tell the newcomers yet about your age?" Chris asked.

Dash shook his head. "I'll tell them in a few days, I promise. Everything is new for them now, I don't want them to worry that the leader Shawn chose might not be able to lead them after all. Anna knows, though. She figured it out."

Chris nodded. "Not much gets by her. She was a powerful opponent, and now you will need her to be a powerful partner."

"I know."

Chris opened his door, and before Dash could react, an arm reached out, grabbed Chris by the shirt collar, yanked him inside, and shut the door.

7

Dash stared at the door in shock. What just happened? He tried to push on the handle, but it didn't budge. Rocket pawed and scratched on the door. He began to whine and then bark, which he almost never did. Chris would never leave Rocket locked outside like this if he was able to open it . . . which could only mean one thing!

Dash lifted his arm to alert the others that Chris was in danger. It turned out he didn't need to. They were all running down the hall toward him.

"What's wrong?" Carly asked, reaching him first. "We heard Rocket barking."

If the situation wasn't so dire, Dash might have laughed. Who needed high-tech arm bands when they had a dog? But the situation *was* dire, so he said, "Colin grabbed Chris and pulled him inside his room! I can't get in!"

Anna tried the door, putting all her strength into it.

"It's no use," Gabriel explained. "The only person who can get in or out of this door is Chris."

Dash cleared his throat. "No. There *is* another way in. I've been there."

The others looked at him in surprise.

Dash leaned against the wall for support as he collected his thoughts. Chris had told him not to tell anyone about his tiny ship, which actually powered the entire *Cloud Leopard*. And also happened to be falling apart. But surely Chris had never expected to be trapped in his own room with his evil clone.

Dash made his decision. "Piper, I'm going to need you to wait here and guard the entrance with Rocket, okay?"

Piper hesitated a second, then nodded. If he picked her specifically, he must have a reason. That was good enough for her.

"Follow me," Dash said to the others, and he ran into the medical bay across the hall. He swiped his finger along the computer screen on the wall beside the portal and set his destination. "We need to get up to the relaxation room. I'll explain there." He jumped in. One by one, the others followed until they were all standing beside him again.

"Aren't we just farther away now?" Anna asked, looking around. "Why'd you bring us up here?"

"Spill," Gabriel said, crossing his arms.

"I was goofing around in the tubes before we left for Tundra," Dash explained as his fingers flew across the navigation screen next to a tube entrance, "and I figured out a new route from here. It dumped me out in a hallway that led to a door I'd never seen before." Dash realized he didn't have to tell them about the tiny ship inside yet. They'd see it for themselves.

"Colin may look like Chris," Anna warned, "but trust me,

from what we've seen here so far, they couldn't be more different. We should move fast."

"I'm trying," he said. Had he turned left after the library, or right?

Gabriel stepped up beside him. "If you took this route before, all you need to do is call up your old log entry."

Relieved, Dash did as he suggested. There it was, the longest one so far.

"Hey, when did that happen? You're in the lead!" Carly said, looking it over. "And you didn't even brag about it?"

"I would have gotten around to it eventually," Dash replied. "Okay, let's go. No one try to go inside the room until we all get there."

Everyone nodded. Dash stepped aside. One by one, they threw themselves into the portal, pressing the saved route each time before jumping. The Omegas couldn't help but squeal with surprise as the twists and turns kept coming. "Wow," Ravi said when he landed at the other end on the cool white floor. "If we'd had sweet rides like that on the *Light Blade,* I might have spent all day in those tubes!"

"Sometimes we do," Carly admitted, landing beside him.

"Everyone good?" Dash asked, the last to arrive. The Omegas nodded, catching their breath. Gabriel and Carly turned in circles, both shocked to have arrived somewhere new on their own ship.

Dash led them toward the near-invisible door in the wall and pointed at the metal strip on the wall that acted as a handle. Gabriel reached for it, but Anna yanked his hand back. "Wait! We need a plan."

"We need to get in there," Gabriel insisted.

"Anna's right," Dash said. "We've learned not to go into battle unprepared."

Gabriel grumbled but lowered his hand.

"Do you think this is going to be a battle?" Siena asked.

"I hope not," Dash said. "I don't know what Colin's capable of, though."

The Omegas exchanged glances. "I'd give this plan making about twenty seconds," Niko said. "Then we get in there either way."

Dash glanced at Anna. "You know Colin better than anyone, right? What do you think is the best way to handle this with the least risk to Chris?"

"And us," Ravi muttered. When they all gave him a look, he held up his hands and said, "What? It's true, right?"

"But you don't *say* it," Siena whispered with an eye roll.

Anna thought for a few seconds. "Colin's not as good as he thinks he is at hiding his agenda. We all knew he would ditch any one of us if it helped him. He tries to hide that, though, by pretending that we're all on the same side and that he's not plotting anything."

Dash considered that. "Okay, how about this. We'll pretend that we're lost and that we just found this door. Chris will know it's not true, but hopefully he'll just go along with it. We'll pretend everything's normal. If Colin doesn't suspect that we're onto him, maybe he'll let his guard down. Then we surround him, edging Chris off to the side to keep him safe."

"What then?" Gabriel asked.

Niko ducked low and put his hands up at face level. "Then we come at him from all sides with all the martial arts training we've had."

The others crouched into various poses—tae kwon do, karate, Krav Maga. With all the giant monster creatures they'd encountered, there hadn't been much use for simple hand-to-hand combat.

"I'm all for trying out my Krav Maga moves on the clone," Ravi said. "But then what? It doesn't seem like Chris can contain him. He must have broken out of whatever holding bay he was keeping him in."

"Maybe he has some kind of on-and-off switch," Carly said, practicing her high kick.

"He's not a robot," Gabriel said.

"I know that," Carly grumbled.

"Are we gonna do this?" Anna asked, pushing Dash toward the door. "Your plan. You make the first move."

Dash took a deep breath. "Here goes." He pulled on the thin metal strip, and the door swung open, just as it had the first time. He stepped inside. The others kept close behind him. ZRKs were everywhere. They seemed agitated, buzzing and zooming in all directions. Dash hadn't seen this many in one place for a long time. He scanned the room quickly but didn't see Chris or Colin. He figured this room must connect to the one Piper was guarding.

"What is this place?" Carly whispered, taking in the bright lights and high ceiling. Her head spun as she tried to figure out how this huge room could be hidden within the ship. Then her eyes scanned down, and she saw the ancient-looking flying machine sitting in the center of the floor. She stopped short. "Holy cow!"

"How is this on our ship and we never knew?" Gabriel asked, his eyes wide.

"I'll explain later," Dash promised. "Right now we need to figure out how this room connects with the locked one. We need to rescue Chris."

"That won't be necessary," a voice said from inside the small ship.

8

Dash stiffened. They all crouched down in their favorite martial arts pose. So much for their surprise attack!

A hatch creaked opened on the side of the ship, and Chris walked out, with Colin right behind him. This was the first time the Alpha crew had seen Colin up close. The two looked identical, except that Colin wore glasses.

Colin spoke first. "I'm sorry if I scared you before, at the door. I just got overexcited to show Chris something I'd figured out about his little ship here."

Chris nodded. "It's going to really boost the power on this thing."

"What *is* this thing?" Carly asked.

Chris explained to everyone what he'd told Dash before. The ship was the one that had carried him from his home planet of Flora, all the way to Earth. Now it powered the *Cloud Leopard*.

Dash only half listened. The others were asking questions about the ship, and he understood their curiosity, but a few seconds ago, they had this whole plan and now it was all for nothing? Chris was acting like he and Colin were the best of buddies. It didn't feel right. Dash looked back and forth between the two. How could they look so alike and yet be so different?

Gabriel must have been thinking the same thing because he said, "Chris, I don't mean to overstep my bounds here, but hello? This guy was made from your DNA—your stolen DNA—and trained to work for your enemy. You're not, like, working together now, are you?"

Chris shrugged. "He's a part of me, whether I like it or not. And I have to admit, in our current stage of the mission, two of me are better than one."

Colin puffed out his chest, looking every bit like a high school football player about to brag that he threw a forty-yard pass. "I'm Chris 2.0," he said with a smirk. "Faster, smarter, and I don't need to sleep."

Chris's smile faltered just a bit. "You don't sleep?"

Colin shook his head, which, Dash now realized, was the tiniest bit larger and squarer than Chris's. Maybe they didn't look exactly alike after all?

"C'mon, guys," Ravi said, heading toward the door. "This reunion is giving me the creeps. Let's go start the movie."

Dash stayed still while the others began to file out of the room. "Are you coming? We're going to watch *Guardians of the Galaxy,*" Gabriel said. "It was Piper's choice. Some of these guys have never seen it. Can you imagine?"

"I'll join you in a minute," Dash said.

"Me too," Anna said.

Niko gave them both a salute. "Bring the popcorn."

"Just ask the snack station for it," Dash said. "It's in the wall of the rec room by the water station."

"Why am I not surprised that your walls make popcorn?" Niko said, shaking his head as he left.

Chris turned to Colin. "Can you finish adjusting the gravitational regulator without me? I need to give them some medical supplies from across the hall."

Without waiting for an answer, Chris ushered Dash and Anna out his front door and straight across the hall to the medical bay. Even without turning around, Dash could tell Colin was watching them walk away. "Is he going to follow us?" Dash whispered as the door to the medical bay slid closed. "He can't leave the room," Chris replied. "My door is programmed to my fingerprint, which, clone or not, he does not share. Well, not once I altered mine when I discovered his existence."

"You don't really trust him, do you?" Anna demanded.

"Keep your friends close and your enemies closer," Chris replied in a low voice.

"Phew," Anna said. "Otherwise I would have said Colin was right, that you aren't very bright."

"You sure you know what you're doing?" Dash asked. "Isn't it dangerous letting him around your old ship?"

"I don't think he'd do anything to risk not getting back home. We will have to be on our guard at the end for any double-crossing, but for now I'd like to think we're on the same side."

Dash looked over his shoulder. "And he's okay staying in your room?"

"For now," Chris said. "I let him have my private quarters, and I'll move into the old ship. There's plenty of room—well, there's enough room—in the back for a cot."

"You know, you've really got to give your ship a name," Dash said. "It deserves something distinguished and powerful, don't you think?"

"Yeah," Anna agreed, "like how about *Rolling Thunder,* or *Sky Wolf,* or the *Freedom of the Stars,* or—"

"It already has a name," Chris admitted, his cheeks growing red.

"What is it?" Dash asked, surprised to see his friend blush. Usually his face was so expressionless.

Chris muttered something and looked away.

"Sorry," Anna said, "what was that again?"

Chris repeated it, only a tiny bit louder. "It's called the *Cloud Kitten.*"

Dash and Anna looked at each other and burst out laughing. Laughing felt good for both of them, and they went on doing it longer than was truly necessary. "Not really the fiercest name," Anna said, wiping a tear away. "You know, for a ship that crossed the universe and back."

"I know that," Chris said. "But Shawn named it when he was a little boy, and it stuck. That's why the transport ship is the *Cloud Cat* and the big mother ship is the *Cloud Leopard.*"

"Ah, I get it," Anna said, just now realizing that Chris had a special bond with the man she knew only as Commander Phillips. She had trouble picturing Phillips as a kid.

"On to more pressing needs," Chris said. He pushed a button

on the wall, and a nearly hidden drawer slid out. It contained the metal box with the serum Dash needed to keep his cells from aging too rapidly. Chris himself used a similar biologic so he could travel through space safely, but because of how his species aged so slowly and uniquely, his injection was different and he only had to take it once so far. If he'd known ahead of time of Dash's situation, he could have come up with a better solution for the boy. As it was, he and Commander Phillips considered themselves lucky that they could get these together in time for the voyage.

Dash grabbed a syringe off the top of the dwindling pile and jammed it into his leg. In all the excitement, he'd actually forgotten he never received it that morning.

Chris pushed the box toward Dash. "With the Colin situation, I don't think it's wise for you to come to my room for these anymore. You'll have to store the shots from now on."

"I could give them to you," Anna offered. "The thought of jabbing Dash with something pointy every day sounds fun!"

"Ha, ha," Dash said dryly. "I'll be just fine on my own. My MTB will remind me or Piper will."

"Spoilsport," Anna said.

"Go catch up with your friends," Chris said. "Try to enjoy yourselves for the next couple of weeks. I'm going to stay in the room a lot working on my ship . . . I mean . . . the *Cloud Kitten*. Now that we're in the final leg of our journey, it's even more important that nothing goes wrong. We can't afford to lose any time at all, not even a day."

Dash and Anna nodded, stepping out into the hall. They were both relieved to see that Colin was no longer in the doorway of Chris's room. "Be careful," Dash said as they left Chris.

"I will," he promised.

When they were far enough away, Dash whispered, *"Cloud Kitten."*

Anna giggled.

He shifted the box from one arm to the other. "I don't think I've heard you giggle before, Anna Turner."

"You tell anyone, I'll deny it."

They ducked into the training center and took the stairs up to the upper floor so Dash could put the box of needles in the boys' dorm. Going through the tunnels with them didn't seem like the smartest idea.

Halfway back to the rec room, Anna murmured, *"Cloud Kitten."*

Now it was Dash's turn to giggle.

9

Usually the weeks spent in Gamma Speed on the *Cloud Leopard* dragged by at a snail's pace. After all, there wasn't much to see. Outside, nothing but streaks of light interrupted the blackness of space as they flew past the stars at an impossible speed.

But those were the old days. Now, with the four Omegas on board, the ship buzzed and hummed with a new energy. After screening *Guardians of the Galaxy* (with nonstop commentary from Gabriel), the group discovered there were a lot of classic alien movies the majority of them hadn't seen. They decided to start weekly movie nights. Each person could choose their own movie to show the others from the seemingly endless supply on board. With eight of them, they figured it would take them right up to their arrival on Dargon. In the five weeks that had passed so far, it had become their favorite group activity. Racing through the tubes and cheering on Anna and Gabriel as they soared side by side in the flight simulators were close seconds (even though Anna usually got too competitive and had to apologize for some of the things she called Gabriel during the flights).

The group clapped as the final credits rolled on Carly's choice. "There," she said, wiping away a stray tear. "Now none of you can say you never saw *E.T.* Did you like it?"

Piper and the boys had seen it already, but Siena and Anna nodded, dabbing at their cheeks.

"I don't think I cried that much since reading *Charlotte's Web* in fourth grade," Siena said.

"Too bad all the real aliens we've met haven't been as cuddly as E.T.," Dash said. "It would make our missions a lot easier." He pulled a heavy sweatshirt over his head, and when he glanced back up, he saw the others were all looking away from him. He wished he'd waited till he got back to the dorm to put it on. He knew what they were thinking. No one wanted to be the one to point out that it wasn't cold in the ship. The ZRKs kept the air at the perfect temperature, and their uniforms also had some kind of technology to help keep them comfortable on board.

The fact that Dash needed an extra layer to keep warm was a reminder that no matter how much fun they were having in Gamma Speed, time was their enemy. Or rather, *his* enemy. He asked Anna to tell Ravi, Niko, and Siena about his condition a few days into the journey. He had run into Ravi first, who said, "Tough break, dude," and gave him an awkward but affectionate pat on the arm. Siena had squeezed his hands and slid over her portion of dessert at dinner. Niko took it the hardest. He'd seemed almost stunned at the thought that their new leader might not live to see the end of their journey. Ever since learning the news, he and Piper had been spending a lot of time together in the medical bay. Dash caught them whispering at other times too. He pretended it didn't bother him, but he hated having people feel sorry for him.

Carly cleared her throat. "I think we should all probably go to bed. Who wants to help me clean up?" She gestured to the array of snacks spread out on the table in front of them. Most of the popcorn bowls only had kernels left in them, and the only sign of the cupcakes Siena made were the crumbs on (and underneath) the table.

"I will," the others all replied at the same time. They jumped up and began carrying bowls or plates or cups out of the rec room. Dash raised a brow at their sudden need for cleanliness and was about to point out that the ZRKs did all the cleaning for them, but the blanket and the darkened room made him yawn instead. Then he was out.

Anna glanced back into the room from the hall. "He's asleep," she whispered to the others.

"At least he made it all the way through the movie this time," Piper said as they scurried down the hall to the kitchen.

"Let's go over everyone's job for tomorrow," Carly said when they were safely out of earshot, in case Dash awoke. "Ravi and Gabe, you have the music lined up?"

Ravi gave a thumbs-up. "STEAM was able to access the list of Dash's favorite songs. We're all loaded up and ready to rock."

"Siena, decorations?"

She nodded. "After lunch, I'll start hanging the streamers. Piper's going to help me reach the high corners."

"Good," Carly said. "Anna, you're set with games?"

Anna nodded. She'd been the one to suggest they go old-school on the games—nothing electronic. Growing up without much money had meant that she'd gotten very good at making up games out of whatever they had lying around the house. Now that Dash's party was getting closer, she was second-guessing it.

"Um, maybe we should just do the usual stuff," she suggested.

"Why?" Carly asked.

Anna shrugged and mumbled, "Maybe my games are dumb and no one will like them."

To her surprise, Gabriel slapped her on the back and said, "Look at you, caring about the enjoyment of others! You're really coming along."

At first, she was annoyed, but the truth of it was hard to ignore. She straightened up. "Hey, I'm Anna 2.0."

They all laughed.

"We're keeping the old-fashioned games," Carly said firmly. "Moving on. Siena and Chris are going to make Dash's favorite desserts. Niko and Piper, you still haven't told us what you're planning?"

The two of them exchanged a glance. "We're putting some finishing touches on it," Piper explained, scooping the last few pieces of popcorn out of the bowl she was clutching.

"Sorry for being secretive," Niko added, but didn't explain further.

Carly was very curious, but she didn't push it. She'd find out soon enough. "And everyone's pretty sure Dash doesn't know about the party?"

"I'm sure Dash doesn't know. He's dreading turning fourteen," Piper said.

Carly nodded. "That's why this party is so important. We have to make it a celebration, not . . ." She trailed off. She'd been about to say, *Not a reminder that every day after that is borrowed time.* They all knew what she was thinking anyway.

10

Dash awoke the following morning in his own bed. It wasn't the first time Chris had to carry him from the couch in the rec room. At first, Dash had been embarrassed about it. Then Chris said something about Piper that Dash couldn't quite hear, but the point had been made. Piper knew when to ask for help. She may not have liked it, but she accepted this was a part of her life. She said thank you and moved on. He would try to do the same.

A glance across the room told him the other boys were already gone, probably halfway through with breakfast already. He knew he should get moving but couldn't make himself pull off the covers. He felt pretty good—physically, at least. Mornings were always the best; nights the worst. He should get up and take advantage of having energy before he felt the inevitable weakening. He still exercised in the training room every morning. But it didn't keep the weakness at bay. Nothing did. The shots kept him alive, but at this point, that was the extent of what they could do.

Fourteen. Such a big number. He didn't expect to be awakened with a Happy Birthday banner stuck on the wall or anything, but somehow he thought the day would feel different. Maybe everyone had forgotten. Or maybe they thought he wouldn't want to celebrate. He certainly hadn't said anything about it.

A knock on the door finally got him to sit up. He swung his legs over the side of the bed and pushed his hair out of his eyes. He waited, expecting one of the boys to walk in. Instead, the knock came again. "Come in," he said.

To his surprise, the door slid open to reveal Piper. The carpet under her chair bent and waved as she floated right above it. He couldn't remember the last time one of the girls had been in the boys' dorm. Piper had her eyes covered with one hand. "Everyone decent?" she asked.

He laughed. "Yup. I should warn you; it's kinda messy in here. I think the ZRKs are trying to teach us a lesson."

She dropped her hand and glanced around at crumpled uniforms, comic books, towels, and random sports equipment littering the floor. "Wow, I think you may be right."

"So . . . ," Dash said. "Are you lost? There are maps of the ship posted in the hallways. I could give you a tour."

She laughed. "Very funny." Then she got serious. "I just came to check on you. It's not like you to miss a meal."

"I'm fine," he said, and jumped up quickly to prove it. He almost whacked his head on Gabriel's bed in the process, but neither of them mentioned it.

"Do you often sleep in your uniform?" she asked.

He looked down at his rumpled clothes. "Apparently I do. Anything else you want to say, or can you leave so I can get dressed?"

"Looks like you already are," she said, stifling a grin. Then she got serious again. "Did you take your injection yet?"

"You're worse than my mom!" Dash said. "I just woke up!"

Piper tapped her foot and crossed her arms. He sighed. Clearly, she wasn't going anywhere until he took it. He had to admit it was nice being so well looked after. It made it easier to bear that they were too far away for Earth to get any messages. It was hard on all of them.

He reached under the bed and slid out the box of prefilled needles. Seeing how few were left was an unnecessary reminder that his time was running out fast. He grabbed one, flicked off the lid, and stuck the small needle into his thigh. When he'd first started taking the serum, he had expected to feel a whoosh of energy go through his body, but it didn't feel like anything at all. If it weren't for the fact that he was still alive on what should have been his last day to survive in space, he wouldn't know the serum was working at all.

Satisfied, Piper turned her chair around and headed for the door.

"You're sure there's nothing else you want to tell me?" Dash called after her. "Nothing at all?" If anyone other than Anna and Chris would know about his birthday, it would be Piper. As the medic, she made it her business to know as much as possible about the crew.

She glanced back at him from the doorway. "Oh, right, there

was something! I meant to tell you that you might want to hurry before Gabriel eats all the pancakes."

She winked as she glided out to the hall. Dash threw a towel at her, but the door had already closed.

Everyone had cleared out of the dining room by the time Dash arrived. Only one plate remained on the table. Someone had covered it with a napkin and written his name on it in blue marker. He pulled the napkin off to reveal one small pancake and a pat of butter. He sighed and told himself it wasn't good to have a full belly when he exercised anyway.

STEAM glided into the room with SUMI hopping in behind him. The two robots were never far apart.

"Hello, Dash," STEAM said. "Would you like us to keep you company?"

Dash swallowed the last bite of pancake. "All done." His stomach rumbled, and he patted it, slightly embarrassed. "Maybe I should ask the ZRKs for something else." He tilted back his head to search the ceiling, which was where the ZRKs usually hung out if they weren't busy cooking or cleaning up dishes. "Hmm, that's weird. I don't think I've ever seen the dining room empty."

"The room is not empty," SUMI said. "We are all in it."

"Yes, SUMI," Dash said patiently. "I meant all the ZRKs seem to be missing."

"I know," SUMI squeaked, and nodded, reminding Dash of the bobblehead baseball player he had on his desk at home. "The ZRKs are not here because they're all in the—"

STEAM reached out one of his robot arms and bonked SUMI

on the head before she could finish her sentence. Dash's eyes widened in surprise, but before he could ask why STEAM did that, the robots hightailed it out of the room.

"That was weird," Dash said to the empty room. He hunted down some juice and a prepackaged nutrition bar, which tasted like cardboard. He ate it anyway. Then he swiped the path on the pad outside the portal and swung himself into the tube. "Huh?" he said out loud as he flew past the curve that he knew would lead him to the training room. He was sure he'd programmed it correctly; he did it every morning. He could do it in his sleep.

The tunnels kept twisting and turning until his body was suddenly propelled out the end. He landed on his butt in a darkened room. He could hear a loud hum and could see three faint glowing spots in the distance, but that was all. Had he found some other hidden area on the ship? Just as he got to his feet, the lights blazed on. He blinked. He was in the rec room! The faint glows were from STEAM, SUMI, and TULIP, standing next to the video game tables.

Before he could ask them what was going on, his attention was drawn upward. A rainbow of streamers hung from the ceiling in large loops. His mouth fell open as he discovered the source of the steady hum. Hundreds—or maybe even *thousands*—of ZRKs buzzed in the air above him. Linked together by their tiny mechanical arms, they formed the words *Happy Birthday, Dash.*

"Wow!" he said, staring up at the amazing sight. He used his MTB to snap a picture of them. This was one image he never wanted to forget. A moment later, the formation disbanded, and the ZRKs went flying off in all directions, leaving only a small portion buzzing in the corners of the room. Dash looked back down and realized the tables were full of pizza and corn dogs and s'mores and basically all his favorite treats from home. The whole crew jumped out from behind the long couch and yelled, "Surprise!"

11

Dash groaned and leaned his head back against the couch cushion. At least this time, it was only a full belly that kept him there. "I can't eat one more bite," he said when Siena handed him the last mini cupcake. "Homemade," she reminded him. "I've been taking lessons."

"I've already eaten four," he insisted.

"Fine," she said, popping it in her mouth. She decided it could have used a pinch more salt and made a mental note to add that to the recipe. She found cooking relaxed her.

Carly came over and sat at the edge of the table. She had a pad and paper in her hand. "I've tallied the results of the games," she announced, "and the winner is—"

At the same time, they all shouted, "Chris!" and turned to look at their alien friend. He had pinned the tail directly on the donkey while blindfolded, had gotten every beanbag in the hole, had gathered the most marbles with his toes, and sailed his paper airplane twice as far as anyone else.

"Me?" Chris said, surprised even though no one else was.

"You earned it, dude," Ravi said. "No one could touch you."

Chris shrugged, a little embarrassed. "I can't help it if my race has uncanny accuracy."

Anna walked over to Chris, reached up, and slipped a chain made out of paper clips over his neck. She'd hung a round cardboard medal from the chain with the word *winner* spelled out in gold stars. She was quite proud of her artwork. Everyone clapped.

Chris lifted the medal and examined it. Then he looked around at the kids' happy faces. He realized that he was going to miss them.

"Are you all right?" Piper asked, peering closely at him.

Chris nodded. He and Shawn had agreed it would be better if he didn't reveal his plans to return to Flora until the end of the mission, when they were certain the kids would make it back to Earth safely. And at this point, he was not the least bit certain of that. Still, he felt terrible not telling them the truth. He looked back down at the handmade medal around his neck and hoped they would forgive him when the time came.

Chris lifted the medal off his chest and slipped it over Dash's head. "Here. A medal is for bravery. You're the brave one; you should have this."

When Dash began to pull it off in protest, Chris said, "I insist. Think of it as a birthday present."

"Gifts!" Carly exclaimed, slapping her forehead. "That's what we forgot!"

"Actually," Piper said, floating forward, "Niko has one. A gift, I mean."

"Totally not necessary," Dash said. "Just being here is the best gift ever."

"I think you'll want this one," Piper said, reaching out to pat Dash on the shoulder.

Niko sat down on the couch and took a deep breath. He glanced up at Piper, who nodded her encouragement. "Okay," he said, then paused and took another deep breath. Then another.

"Um," Dash said, "are you all right? You really don't need to give me anything."

When Niko still didn't say anything, Piper swung herself out of her chair and sat down on Dash's other side. "Niko's gift," she said. "It's the gift of healing."

Dash looked from Piper to Niko, then back again. "Say what now?"

"When I first got to the *Light Blade,* Niko was almost dead from the Stinger poison," Piper told the group. "Anna had brought some antidote serum from the planet's surface, but—"

"We saw that stuff," Carly said. "Colonel Ramos said it was practically useless. Guess it would have been smart to take it just in case." She glanced at Anna with what might have been the first sign of approval she'd ever given her.

"Anyway," Piper continued, "the antidote did lower his fever a bit, but it wasn't formulated for humans, so it wasn't strong enough to knock out the poison on its own."

Niko reached over and took Piper's hand and squeezed it. He knew he should be the one telling the story now. "So Piper kept asking me questions about my childhood to keep me talking. I remember feeling so cold and talking about how my mother told me I had this healing power." He paused to look at the skeptical looks on his friends' faces. "It's not like I can touch someone and they're instantly well again," he rushed to say. "Well, sort of. My great-great-grandmother was a healer of sorts—back then, the people in her village thought she used magic, but really it's just acupressure."

"Acupressure?" Dash asked. "What's that?"

"It's a form of therapy. Basically, we find a specific point on the body and apply pressure in order to treat pain or a specific ailment," Niko explained. "The Japanese call it *shiatsu*."

Chris pulled out his notebook and began scribbling madly.

Piper spoke up, her words coming in a rush. "Dash, Niko can help you. I know it sounds crazy, but I swear Niko's hands really are like magic." Niko blushed.

"He can't replace the shots you take," Piper explained. "Or give you more time in general, but he can give you more energy. We've been experimenting together on my legs. I'll never be able to move them, but the rest of my body is more energized, which means I can do more. The only downside is that it doesn't last long. But we figured if he practices this acupressure on you each day until we reach Dargon, you'll have enough energy to go with the ground team!"

Dash's eyes grew wide. He turned to Niko. "You're sure it will work?"

Niko nodded. "I'm sure. You're our best hope for success; everyone knows it. Plus," he continued, "as the captain, you should be there for the last adventure." He glanced at the others. Everyone nodded in agreement, except for Anna. She hesitated a second longer than the others, but eventually gave a grunting nod.

Dash looked around the room at his friends—human, alien, and robot. He knew they felt sorry for him, but they'd made today a celebration—Carly had even played her guitar for them, which she never did—and now they'd actually given him something to celebrate. He grinned. "When do we start?"

12

The next few weeks sped by faster than anyone wanted. Niko poured all his energy into Dash's healing treatments—and they were proving to be a great success!

Dash was very grateful for the extra energy, especially since Chris was making them train pretty hard for the conditions they'd face on Dargon. Chris's notes from his visit to the planet were in the library, and Siena and Carly spent a lot of time researching the species the ground team would meet there. They'd taught the others a few customs and traditions to help make them seem more trustworthy when they first approached them. One of the weirder ones was that they'd have to approach the elves backward, while whistling, to prove their visit was peaceful. They'd all spent a lot of time practicing their best whistles, until Chris told them it was giving him a headache and they had to stop.

The evening before they were scheduled to leave Gamma Speed, Chris called a meeting to go over the last-minute details. Everyone had been so busy on board the huge ship, that the eight of them were rarely all together in one room other than meals and movie nights. Dash hoped the meeting wouldn't go too long—it was finally going to be his turn to show his favorite alien movie.

Chris stood at the head of the table and clasped his hands together. "I am going to tell you the story of my visit to Dargon. Admittedly, before some of your other trips I wasn't fully forthcoming with what I knew about the planet."

"You can say that again," Piper said. "Especially on Meta Prime! Knowing you'd created a giant video game and were plopping us in the middle might have been nice."

"Wait, you guys didn't know that?" Anna asked.

The Alpha team shook their heads and glared a bit at Chris.

"Don't forget Infinity," Carly said. "A heads-up that we may have become permanent guests on the planet wouldn't have hurt."

Dash bounced in his seat. "Or on Aqua Gen, those Thermites were way more vicious than you—"

Chris held up his hand. "Okay, okay, I get it. Some details were news to me too. And others, well, I didn't always know whether it would be helpful or harmful for you to have too much background on my own experience, knowing it could just distract from retrieving the elements. But this time you need to know the whole story or retrieving the element will be impossible. You already know the basics—the ogres, elves, and dragons that inhabit this world."

They nodded, leaned back in their chairs and waited.

"When I visited Dargon about a hundred years ago, the ogres were constantly attacking the elves, burning their ancient, hollowed-out trees just for sport. The trees aren't simply the spiritual center of life for the elves; they are their homes. But the ogres can't burn the trees on their own; they taunt the dragons, whose fiery hot breath burns the trees."

Carly raised her hand. "So it wasn't the dragons' fault that the trees burned; it was really the ogres?"

Chris nodded. "Although of course the elves retaliated in kind. Can't really blame them. The element I needed—that you will now need to retrieve as well—is made from the embers of a burnt tree root. They would not agree to part with any piece of the tree until I came up with a plan they couldn't refuse."

Everyone leaned forward in their seats now.

"During my time on the planet, I'd discovered that the ogres were very sensitive to sounds. There was one tone that seemed to put them into almost a trance state. It took many weeks, but I was able to construct a special horn that would produce the exact tone I needed. If sounded once, it would put any ogre who heard it to sleep. The same sound would also wake them up. The plan would be to put the ogres to sleep and leave the horn with the elves, who would keep it safe. As happy as I'm sure they are with their peaceful existence without the ogres, I made the elves promise to protect the horn from destruction. They know a day will come when the horn will have to be played again. Tomorrow is that day."

"So let me get this right," Ravi said. "First we have to get the elves to agree to let us sound the horn and awaken the evil ogres, then hope the ogres make the dragons so angry they breathe fire on the houses of the elves? And then we just walk away with a piece of the wreckage?"

"Not a lot can go wrong *there,*" Gabriel muttered under his breath.

Ignoring Gabriel's comment, Chris nodded to Ravi. "Sounds about right."

Ravi's shoulders slumped. "Well, that doesn't seem like much fun."

"Especially for the elves," Piper said. "We have to burn their house down."

"I even feel a little sorry for the ogres," Siena said. "Who gave you the right to decide to put them to sleep like that? No disrespect intended."

Chris opened his mouth to reply, then closed it again. He sighed. "I hear you, I do. But these ogres were really awful. It brought peace to the land and no doubt saved many elves' lives, not to mention the ancient trees."

Carly stood up and started pacing. "What if we skip the whole thing with the ogres and the dragons, and just set the tree on fire ourselves? I mean, with the elves' permission, of course."

Chris shook his head. "Believe me, if I could take the dragons out of the equation I would. Unfortunately, only the dragons have fire hot enough to burn the wood to reach the root, and only the ogres can find them. The combination of a dragon's breath and the material in the tree is what provides the element we need. It's called dragon cinder. Best-case scenario would be that the ogres only awaken one dragon. They are solitary creatures who hate everything else that moves on the planet, even each other."

Carly sighed and sat back down.

"It was worth a try," Gabriel said, patting her on the arm.

"What if the elves don't want us to sound the horn?" Dash asked. "We could be out of the game before we even start."

"Don't worry about that," Chris said. "I warned them that I would be back again one day and we'd need to reawaken them. They agreed, making me promise that after the next trip, I would take the horn far away from the planet, and the ogres would sleep forever. I fully plan to uphold my end of the bargain."

"So you're going with us?" Dash asked.

"Yes. As on Infinity, I think having me on the ground with you will be an asset to the mission," Chris answered.

The crew exchanged glances. They weren't convinced that it would be that easy—and what about Colin? They couldn't just leave him alone on the *Cloud Leopard.* There was no telling what he might do! Chris could feel their skepticism. He needed to turn this around. He planted a smile on his face and said, "On the positive side, there will be more manpower than—"

"Manpower?" Siena, Anna, Carly, and Piper said at the same time.

Chris stopped talking and looked at them. "Um, manpower and lady power?"

Carly and Siena wrinkled their noses.

Chris tried again. "Girl power? Woman power?"

"Better," Piper said with a nod. "Go on."

"As I was saying," Chris continued with a sigh, "you'll have more man and woman power than ever before. Plus, you'll have four days on the surface of the planet, much longer than at our other stops. I had to build in the extra time to get the ogres up the cliffs to find the dragons. They move very slowly."

"Who is going to be on the ground team?" Carly asked. "Besides you and Dash, I mean."

Chris glanced at Dash before answering. "We talked it through very carefully. We'd like Carly and Anna to remain on board as cocaptains in Dash's absence. Carly will continue to monitor the source machine and prepare it for the dragon cinder."

Carly nodded, not looking at Anna. Anna slumped in her seat.

"Ravi and Niko will man the *Cloud Cat,* delivering anything necessary to the team on the surface. Niko will also continue his duties as medic on board."

Ravi and Niko high-fived each other. "That's cool," Ravi said, "even though I totally have the best whistle out of everyone." It was true. He could blow out whole melodies, and they actually sounded like the real songs.

"I'm sure the elves will still welcome us without your contribution," Siena said.

Ravi grinned. "Maybe they will; maybe they won't."

"Moving on," Chris said. "Piper will go to the surface, along with Gabriel and Siena."

Piper grinned. She'd missed going on the missions.

Dash was glad that no one was complaining about their assignments. With so many crew members, the choice had been difficult. Before Chris could turn away from the table, Dash said, "There's something you haven't told us."

Chris froze. There were actually a few things he hadn't told them. Which one was he referring to?

Dash hesitated. A few weeks ago, he wouldn't have asked this in front of the others, but now he felt comfortable enough and he was sure they'd want to know the answer too. "You said we'll need four days on the planet, but I only have four days left before I run out of serum. Right?"

Chris nodded. He relaxed a bit when he realized where Dash was going with this.

"I don't understand how it can take us only one day to get home," Dash said, "when it took us a year to get here?"

"It won't take you one day to get home," Chris replied.

"It won't?" the others said together.

Chris shook his head and smiled. "It will take one *second*."

13

Chris walked back toward his room, Rocket at his heels. The dog had taken to following him everywhere over the last few days, as if he knew they were soon to part ways.

He ran the briefing through his head to make sure he hadn't left out any important details. He hoped his description of how the Source worked was clear enough. He'd tried to explain that once the elements were mixed, the power would be so great that even a tiny amount could punch a four-dimensional hole through space-time that would send the ship back to Earth almost instantly. They all acted like they understood, but they were also anxious to enjoy their last evening in Gamma Speed, so he couldn't be entirely sure.

He picked up his pace. He didn't like leaving Colin alone for too long. He hadn't told the kids how difficult it had been these last two months keeping the clone out of trouble. More than once he'd caught him trying to patch into the communication system to get a message to Ike Phillips. And, once, Colin had managed to override the force field that kept him in the room. Chris had caught it with one second to spare. He was very glad the mission was almost over so he wouldn't have to deal with Colin anymore.

Chris had almost reached his room, when he felt something shift in the air around him. It was almost imperceptible, the slightest change in the hum that ran through the floors and walls, such a constant that no one ever noticed it anymore. Until it stopped.

Chris broke into a run.

Back in the rec room, the crew settled into the couches to watch their last movie of the trip. While the ZRKs were flying in and out depositing bowls of snacks on the table, Siena took the opportunity to pull Dash aside.

"I was just wondering," she began, then hesitated. Dash and the others had made her feel welcome from the start, but there was no denying that she still felt ashamed of her actions while on the *Light Blade*. As a result, she'd kept a lower profile than the others had. She took a deep breath and tried again. "I was just wondering why you chose me for the ground crew. I mean, I want to go and all."

Dash answered right away. "You're fast, you're smart, and you're good with a sword."

She looked at him with surprise. "You know about my fencing?" She'd been practicing at night sometimes, running through training simulations when the others went to bed. It calmed her down and made her feel stronger.

He smiled. "It's a big ship, but not *that* big."

She smiled back, tentatively at first, but then with genuine affection. For the first time in a long time, she was looking forward to being needed.

Suddenly, Chris's voice boomed through the ship. "Brace yourselves! We're leaving Gamma Speed in ten seconds. Nine . . . eight . . ."

There was no time to ask what was going on. Their hearts in their throats, the crew scrambled to the simulation machines, pairing off two per seat. The robots—who always watched the movies with them—hooked their arms around the base of the seats. Piper pulled her chair up beside Dash's seat, and he looped the seat belt around her. He'd just clicked it closed when Chris's voice said, "Zero. Brace for impact." The ship wobbled and shook violently for what felt like forever before finally grinding to a screeching halt. Their heads flew back against the headrests, making more than one person groan.

"Is everyone okay?" Dash shouted, throwing off his straps. Groans and yeses came back. He did a quick check of the crew. Pale and shaken, but in one piece.

"You were right," Anna said, rubbing her neck. "Leaving Gamma really was a lot worse than going into it."

Dash pressed at his Mobile Tech Band with shaking fingers. "Chris! Come in! Why are we out of Gamma already? What's going on? Did we arrive at Dargon early?" He waited for a reply but only got silence. The crew exchanged looks of alarm. "Chris!" Dash tried again. "Can you hear me?"

Still silence. The rec room didn't have any windows, so they couldn't tell if the planet lay below them or not.

Finally, the intercom crackled to life. "Crew to the flight deck" was all Chris said before cutting out again. It took a second for everyone to move. They'd heard Chris sound anxious before, even fearful. But they'd never heard him sound defeated.

14

"I don't understand," Dash said, pacing back and forth in front of the long, curved window that currently revealed nothing but black space. No suns, and definitely no planet Dargon. "How could Colin have done this?" He raked his fingers through his hair, over and over until it stood on end. This used to soothe him when his mom did it. It wasn't working now. The others paced right along with him.

"I don't know," Chris admitted. He sat in his usual seat on the flight deck, shoulders slumped, his face expressionless. "He must have planned this with Ike."

"He got through to Earth?" Carly asked, stopping short and causing Anna to bump right into her, and Ravi to bump right into Anna.

"Maybe," Chris said miserably. "Or maybe this was their plan from the beginning." He put his hands on both sides of his head. "He used my own memories, my own knowledge. He knew we'd be stuck here."

"It's not your fault," Dash said. "There's no way Ike and Colin knew the *Light Blade* was going to catch fire. And you didn't create Colin. You're as much a pawn in all this as we are." Once the words were out, he wished he could take them back. The hurt on Chris's face was clear.

"Is that how you feel?" Chris asked, looking around the room. "Like you're being manipulated or tricked?"

They all exchanged glances. Piper floated forward. "Maybe in the beginning," she admitted. "For one thing, we were told we were on a mission to one planet, not six."

Chris sighed. "I know. We were afraid no one would go on the mission if they knew how truly dangerous it was. And the mission is so important. Your whole world is only years away from total darkness. We had to weigh the risk of keeping things from you against the reward of coming back with the Source."

"We don't have to like it, but we understand," Dash said. He needed to get Chris's focus back on their current situation. "So where is Colin now?"

"Vulcan death grip?" Ravi guessed.

Chris just stared at him and shook his head. "Locked in my quarters again," he answered.

"Okay, then. What does coming out of Gamma too early mean for the mission?" Dash asked.

"Can't we just go back into Gamma Speed?" Ravi said.

Chris shook his head. "We had only enough material for one burst between each planet. That's why we would have needed the Source to get us home. Even so, I did try to restart when the ship first shut down."

"How fast can this thing move under its own propulsion?" Anna asked.

"Honestly, not fast," Chris admitted. "The *Cloud Leopard* was never meant to fly long distances at normal speeds. So far, it's only gone from Earth up to where we boarded. We are a lot farther away from Dargon than that."

Gabriel stepped away from the control panel, which he'd been studying carefully since they got up there. "According to my calculations, we're about three days' journey away from Dargon now. If we could get this thing moving . . ." He trailed off. They all knew the answer, though. They didn't have three days.

"You're forgetting something," Anna told Chris. "You have some of the best engineering minds of their generation in front of you. And some pretty smart robots. You need to snap out of this funk you're in and focus. What's the least amount of time we can spend on Dargon and still have a chance of getting the element?"

"Four days," Chris mumbled.

Anna repeated the question, more forcefully this time.

"Two?" he offered, not even sounding remotely confident.

Anna turned to face the crew. "We will have to be resourceful and think outside the box. Failure is—"

"Not an option!" the crew shouted. Even the robots joined in.

"That's right," she said firmly, her hands on her hips. "We have two days max to get this hunk of metal to Dargon. Let's get to work."

It was now clear to Dash why Ike Phillips had chosen Anna to be the captain of the *Light Blade*. She may be bossy and demanding, but when not under Colin and Ike's control, she proved able to get everyone to keep from freaking out about being stuck in the cold, dark depths of space. Of course, she did this mainly by cutting off anyone midsentence who had begun to express worry or doubt, but still, her method was effective.

Chris explained that the amount of fuel left in the *Cloud Leopard*'s engines would only be enough to get them closer by one day. That left two days in which they'd be stuck drifting in space. That was two days they didn't have.

"Whatever happened to saving some fuel for a rainy day?" Ravi muttered. "This ship has duplicates, sometimes triplicates of every item, and we have enough food to last for at least five more years, you'd think they might have thought ahead about carrying some extra fuel."

"It took us a decade to put together enough for the mission," Chris explained, a bit put off. Then he sighed. "But I see your point. I'll be sure to mention it to Shawn the next time we have to plan a mission to the far reaches of the universe to keep a planet from dying."

Carly elbowed Chris. "Sarcasm suits you."

The group smiled. It was a short-lived moment of amusement, but it was better than nothing. They split up and got to work.

Gabriel and Ravi began investigating the engines of the *Cloud Kitten,* convinced they could get it to work on less fuel than it had been using. STEAM and SUMI calculated how much material would be needed to give them even the shortest of bursts.

It occurred to Carly that now that they had so many of the elements just sitting in the Element Fuser, couldn't they use some of them to reenter Gamma Speed? After all, if the fuel was made from chemicals that were supposed to mimic the elements, why not use the real deal?

But when she asked him, Chris shook his head. "Those all need to go into making the Source. We can't afford to dip into any of them. Clearly, they are not replaceable at this point." He had spent the last few decades of his life working toward collecting those elements; he would never risk anything happening to them.

"But if we can't get to Dargon, there won't *be* a Source to make," Carly pointed out.

"I'm sorry, the answer's no," he said, and went back to fiddling with the communication system. He hadn't given up on trying to reach Shawn, even though he knew that radio waves could never reach that far, not in time to help them, anyway.

"I think it's a good idea," Anna whispered to Carly.

Carly knew Chris was right when he said they'd need all the elements to create the Source in the end. Still, she had determined that only three elements with even the tiniest amount to spare might help. When combined, the elements wouldn't get them into Gamma Speed, but it could give them a boost so the *Cloud Leopard* could fly faster.

With Anna and Siena's help, Carly collected a centigram of Rapident Powder, 1/230 of an ounce of liquid metal from TULIP's belly (which made the slogger giggle as it was extracted), and a milligram of the zero crystals from Tundra. "So that's what those were supposed to look like," Anna murmured, admiring the shiny crystals. Siena brought them all to the lab, where she scanned them in to identify their chemical compositions, then carefully carried everything down to the *Cloud Kitten.*

Gabriel's eyes lit up when he saw the three elements and the results of Siena's analysis. He entered the data into the ship's ancient computer, then fed the elements into the engine. He ran back to the control panel and checked the gauges. The needles wobbled but quickly fell back to zero. They really needed more solid material. "Almost there," he said, trying to sound more optimistic than he felt.

"Maybe Niko can send some of his magic energy into the engine," Ravi said, only half joking.

"Where is Niko, anyway?" Siena said, looking around. "I haven't seen him in hours."

"Here I am!" Niko said, running into the room. Panting, he held out his hand to reveal a box of playing cards.

"Pretty sure we don't have time for a game of Go Fish," Gabriel said.

Niko shook his head. "It's my Stinger spore! I mean, the one that hit me. Days later, I found it wedged into the lining of the shirt I'd worn on the Infinity mission."

Gabriel reached out for it excitedly. "And you kept it?"

Niko nodded. "I thought it would make a perfect good-luck charm."

"It didn't give us much luck on the *Light Blade,*" Anna reminded him, "but everything deserves a second chance, right?" And every*one,* she thought.

"This is perfect," Gabriel said, tipping the box over until the tiny pellet dropped into a narrow tube that snaked around into the engine. It clinked as it hit the sides and then was heard no more. "The only thing we need now is a catalyst," he said, eyes red with exhaustion. "Some kind of liquid that will fuse the molecular bonds of the different elements."

After a few seconds of silence, Piper took a deep breath. "What about Dash's serum?"

Everyone turned to her expectantly.

She wished she didn't have to say it. Saying it would make it real. But she heard Chris's voice in her head lecturing them about risk versus reward. Which was greater here? How could she choose? In a voice barely above a whisper, she said, "Dash's serum. It could be your catalyst. You'd only need one vial of it."

"But that would mean he'd lose one more day," Carly said, her stomach twisting into a knot. "He only has three left."

Piper closed her eyes. "I know."

15

"**You ask him,**" Anna urged Piper. "You two have always had a special bond or whatever. Since back at the base."

Piper shook her head. "I can't do it. Carly, you ask. You're his second-in-command."

"No way." She turned to Gabriel. "How about you?" she asked him. "You know, man to man."

Gabriel shifted his weight and looked around the room. "I vote for Niko. He has that calm, Zen thing going for him. Dash would—"

"No one needs to ask me." Dash's voice came out of nowhere. "I'll do it." The group collectively jumped and whirled around before realizing the voice was coming from Siena's arm.

"Guys?" he repeated when no one spoke. "Can you hear me? I'm on an open channel on Siena's MTB."

Carly cleared her throat, embarrassed. "Guess you heard our conversation?"

"Yup," the voice said.

They all looked at Siena accusingly. "Sorry!" she whispered, shaking the arm with the MTB. "Still haven't gotten the hang of this thing."

"Dash," Piper said, "you don't have to do this. We can find another way." She looked over at Gabriel hopefully.

He shook his head and mouthed the word *no*.

Piper grimaced. "Well, maybe we can't, but that doesn't mean you have to—"

"Yes," Dash interrupted. "It does. Remember you said that as bad as it was, you were supposed to be on the *Light Blade* in order to save their whole crew when the ship started to burn?"

Piper looked down. "Yes, but—"

"This is just like that," Dash said firmly. "This is something only *I* can do. If I wasn't on board, if I didn't need the serum, we'd be stuck here."

Piper didn't reply. What more could she say?

A ZRK flew down with Dash's injection a minute later. Gabriel emptied the fluid into the funnel, sealed the lid to the engine tight, and said, "Step back."

"What now?" Piper asked, zooming backward.

"Now it has to heat nearly as high as the surface of the sun."

While the crew worked to get the ship moving again, Colin paced the small space of Chris's room. He'd had a small victory when he pulled the ship out of Gamma Speed. The plan wasn't to sabotage the mission completely, only to delay it long enough to weaken the crew completely. Then Colin could return to Earth the sole champion. He'd get all the glory. And he'd figure out what to do about Chris later.

For now, though, Colin was trapped, and he hated being trapped. He tore some ancient-looking books off a shelf and sat down with the intention of ripping the pages out—anything so long as it was destructive. But when he flipped the largest tome open, a picture caught his eye. It was an illustration of a plant, something called the Walla-nika plant. Colin recognized it. He'd seen a small sample of its leaves stored in a trunk in Chris's room. The leaves were kept in a large glass bottle with what looked like a warning label slapped on the front. Without reading, Colin knew the plant came from the shallow waters of a planet called Flora. And that it could be deadly. But how did he know that? Colin felt the tug of a smile at the corner of his lips.

Sharing Chris's memories had been a blessing and a curse. But this memory was by far Colin's favorite.

Fifteen minutes later, all eight members of the crew converged on the flight deck. When Chris had learned they had enhanced the fuel, his face at first showed no expression, which for him wasn't out of the ordinary. His eyes opened wide, and he finally broke out of the daze he'd been in. "How?"

The crew exchanged glances, and then Carly spilled out the whole story. Chris's face darkened when he heard the part about using the elements. Carly assured him they would still have enough to make the Source. Finally, Chris relaxed. He went to

Dash's seat and grasped him on the shoulder. "I'm reminded why Shawn put you in charge instead of me. I'm sorry for doubting you. All of you. I haven't handled the Colin problem very well. I should have taken him off-line when he first came on board. I just . . . it felt . . . confusing."

"Don't feel bad," Ravi said. "If we all had evil clones, I'm sure we would have handled it a lot worse."

"So this means we'll arrive at the planet just one day behind schedule?" Chris asked.

"According to my calculations, yes," Gabriel confirmed.

Chris nodded. "I'm beyond proud of all of you. Your actions will go down in history." He paused. "But now we've got to focus on the mission."

"Of course," Dash said, hopping up from his seat. "We're all packed and as prepared as we're ever gonna be."

"And the *Cloud Cat* is juiced up and ready to go," Gabriel added. "We can leave as soon as we arrive in orbit."

"Only if it's daytime on the planet," Chris replied.

"Shouldn't they go no matter when it is?" Anna asked. "We've lost so much time already."

Chris shook his head. "You wouldn't want to approach the elves while they're sleeping, or the ogres either, for sure. We've lost a full day on the planet, so at the end of the third day, we'll have to have the Source ready or else Dash will not get back in time."

Piper took a deep breath and said, "Actually . . . we'll only have two days there. We had to use one of Dash's vials to bond the elements we used."

Chris winced, like the news physically hurt him. He shut his eyes. Piper and Dash exchanged a concerned look. When he opened them again, he wouldn't meet Dash's gaze.

"I'll work on a new plan," he said in an even tone, "and will load it to your Mobile Tech Bands by morning. You should know that when the horn on Dargon was blared, the sound waves continuously circled the planet. This is what keeps the ogres asleep, but it will keep our radio signals from getting through. We will be on our own down there for a while. For now, you should all get much needed sleep, and I will wake you when we arrive. Good night." He quickly left the flight deck with Rocket trotting obediently after him.

"Is it just me," Ravi said, "or did he seem mad?"

"Not just you," Carly said.

"At least he's not in zombie mode anymore," Dash said. "That was pretty creepy."

Piper glided toward the door. "We better do what he said."

No one felt much like sleeping, but as soon as their heads hit the pillows, they were out. The next thing they knew, they were being flung to the floor.

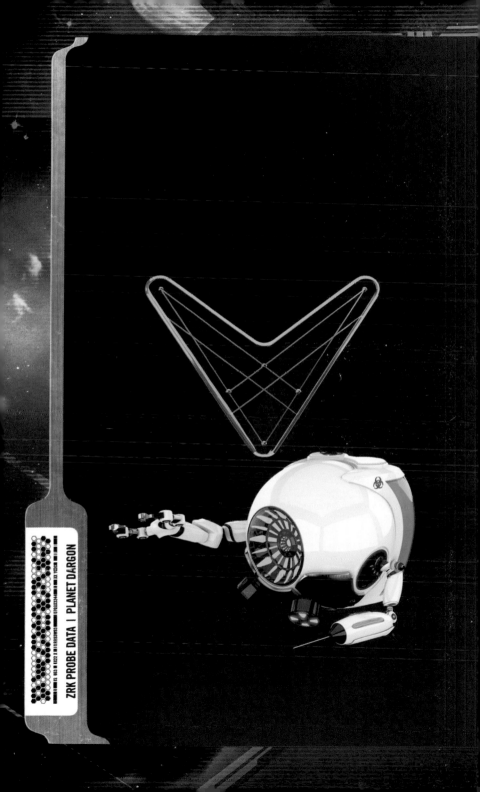

I K JGX 1862 K 1179166X0M 4270E3RE3 2C 2080

TOP-SECRET MISSION BRIEF

UNCHARTED OUTPOST – PLANET FLORA

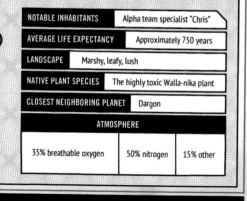

NOTABLE INHABITANTS	Alpha team specialist "Chris"
AVERAGE LIFE EXPECTANCY	Approximately 750 years
LANDSCAPE	Marshy, leafy, lush
NATIVE PLANT SPECIES	The highly toxic Walla-nika plant
CLOSEST NEIGHBORING PLANET	Dargon

ATMOSPHERE		
35% breathable oxygen	50% nitrogen	15% other

16

"**What's going on?**" Dash shouted into his MTB. It took all his strength to hold on to the leg of his bed as his own legs flew up behind him. The metal box with the last two injections slid out from under the bed. It barely missed Dash's head and slammed into his shoulder instead. Gabriel and Niko had been tossed from their upper bunks and were grasping the carpet with all their strength. Ravi had managed to crawl back up onto his bed and gripped the sides with both hands.

"Hold tight!" Chris's voice boomed through the intercom system. "The ship wasn't programmed for the extra burst we had to give it. I thought it would tell us when we arrived in orbit but obviously not. Ten more seconds."

The ship stopped bucking and swaying as suddenly as it started.

Dash sat up, rubbing his shoulder. "Everyone okay?"

"Still in one piece," Niko replied, rolling over onto his back in the carpet.

"Well, that's one way to get us out of bed," said Gabriel.

Ravi groaned and sat up. "I think I prefer my alarm clock."

"I'm going to check on the girls," Dash said. When he reached the hall, he heard what sounded like crying and knocked hard on the door.

"Come in!" Anna called.

He quickly pushed the button, and the door slid open. He'd expected to find the girls in similar positions to how he'd left the boys. Instead, they were all hanging on to Piper's chair, hovering three feet off the floor! What had sounded to him like crying was actually laughing!

"Did it stop?" Carly asked, spotting him. "We can't feel it in the air."

Dash shook his head in astonishment. "Yes, it stopped."

Piper lowered the chair, and the three girls hopped off.

"Glad to see someone was having fun," Dash said. "I didn't even know your chair could hold that much weight."

"SUMI made some modifications," Piper explained. "It also does this." She turned a knob on the arm of the chair. LED lights flashed on and off around her head, and a Beyoncé song that had been popular when they'd left Earth blared out of speakers by each shoulder blade.

"Nice!" Dash shouted above the noise.

The other boys ran in at that point. "You guys having a party in here and didn't invite us?" Ravi asked.

Chris walked in at that moment, took in the scene, and quickly assessed there were no broken bones. He cleared his throat. "We have arrived in Dargon's orbit," he said. "We are fortunate in that it is still early morning on the planet below, so you can get down there right away. Your updated instructions have been uploaded. You should know that the crews have been adjusted slightly." Everyone looked at each other. What did *that* mean?

"Needless to say," Chris continued, "you will now have much less time to gain the elves' trust and much less time setting the plan into action once the ogres wake up. I'd advise everyone get dressed."

Chris turned around and left the room.

"Wait. You're not going with us now, are you?" Dash asked, following Chris down the hall.

Chris looked away and shook his head. "It's Colin."

"What about him? Isn't he locked in your room?"

Chris bit his lip. "He's not."

"Then where is he?" Dash asked.

"That's just it. I don't know."

Dash didn't know what to say. How could Chris not know where Colin was? This was bad. Really bad.

"How did he escape?" Dash asked.

"I think he had help."

"Help? From who?" Everyone had been working together, even Anna. Dash couldn't think of anyone that might want to help Colin.

Chris didn't answer. Instead, he said, "I think Anna may need to join you as part of the ground crew—at least until I find Colin."

"You think Anna helped him?" Dash was shocked. Then

again, this was Anna they were talking about. She had done some pretty sneaky things in the past.

"Don't tell the others," Chris said. "I'm not sure. I just need a little time. Tell everyone they're going in the *Cloud Cat* to see the ground crew off. It should be enough time for me to find him."

Dash looked Chris directly in the eyes. "I hope so," he said. "Or we're done for."

After wolfing down breakfast, the Voyagers sped through the tubes to the engine room. Dash had the final syringe tucked away in his backpack and was doing his best not to think about it. He chose instead to think about how the inhabitants of the planet below them had no idea their lives were about to change.

Chris made it seem that he was agreeing to let everyone accompany the ground team down to the planet. Dargon would be the last planet the crew would ever visit, he explained. It had a special significance that the other planets hadn't. Only Dash knew the truth.

"I have one more surprise for you," Chris said once they were all assembled in the engine room.

"You promised no more surprises," Dash reminded him.

"You'll like this one." Chris led them through the cavernous engine room, past the Element Fuser and the area where the planetary vehicles used to sit, most of them abandoned on different planets. None of the crew had a reason to come down to this end of the room since they'd left Tundra.

"Meet your new planetary vehicle." Chris dramatically

pulled a sheet off what looked like a steel box with small windows and thick wheels. Dash rapped his knuckles on the side of the vehicle. "This looks like a tank."

"It *is* a tank," Chris said. "But without the turret and guns. The ZRKs have been working on it the past two months."

"Couldn't they have built another hovercraft?" Gabriel asked. "I was hoping to race Piper."

"It wouldn't help you down there," Chris said. "You can't outrun the elves in a hovercraft. And you can't outmaneuver the ogres. This tank will protect you at nighttime, and if you find yourself in danger."

Chris pulled Dash to the side as the others headed back to the *Cloud Cat*. "Be careful down there," he warned him. "No one is likely to take kindly to strangers appearing from the sky. Remember the order—elves first, then ogres, dragons."

"We got this," Dash promised. "And I feel good, so don't worry about me."

"I'm going to worry anyway," Chris said, sticking out his hand.

Dash shook it. "I'll see you tomorrow." He started to pull his hand away when Chris said, "The elves, they may not let—"

"C'mon, Dash," Gabriel said, sticking his head out of the back of the transport ship. "Clock's ticking."

"Coming," Dash said, hesitating one more second to give Chris a chance to finish what he'd been saying. But Chris just stepped back and waved, as though relieved he had gotten interrupted.

If felt a little strange for Gabriel to hand the controls of the *Cloud Cat t*o someone else, but he knew his replacement was more than capable. For his part, Ravi wanted to impress Gabriel and worked really hard to make sure the ride was smooth. Ravi let out a breath of relief when he set the ship down only a few feet from where Chris had instructed. "Nice," Gabriel said, high-fiving him.

The crew spilled out, gasping at the beauty of the wildflower-filled valley and the majestic forest spread before them. The forest wasn't scary or forbidding, like the deep jungle of J16 had been, just very, very beautiful. Enormous—both in width and height—trees reached toward the sky. Moss-covered rocks the size of trucks dotted the landscape. "Total LOTR!" Gabriel said excitedly to Ravi.

"Total!" Ravi agreed.

"LOTR?" Carly asked.

"Lord of the Rings," Anna replied with an eye roll.

But she *totally* agreed. She almost expected to see a hobbit walk out of the lush woods. The breeze carried a faint salty smell from an ocean too far away to see. The air smelled woodsy and alive, a smell that was decidedly missing from both the *Light Blade* and the *Cloud Leopard.* In fact, unless Chris was making one of his special meals, there were practically no smells on board the spaceships at all. She breathed in deep again, hoping some of it would accompany her back up.

Carly flopped down on the thick, soft grass and stared up at the blue-purple sky. "I wonder if this is what Earth was like, you know, before people. All wild and peaceful."

"It won't be peaceful for long," Piper said, looking up at the sky. "Not when the ogres and dragons come along."

"Dragons?" Niko said, bending his neck backward to look up. "Did someone say dragons?"

"Relax, dragon boy," Siena said. "They're not out yet."

"Rats," Niko said.

"I'll try to take a picture for you," she offered, patting him on the arm.

"Try to get one face-on," he said excitedly, "and then a profile, and if you can get an action shot with him, you know, actually setting something on fire, that would be great."

Siena stared at him. "Sure, I'll ask the ferocious fire-breathing dragon to pose for me."

"You're a pal," Niko said, grinning.

"All right, guys," Anna said, checking her MTB. "We've got to let them get to it. Those ogres aren't gonna wake themselves."

Carly gave everyone hugs, then climbed back into the *Cloud Cat* with Anna. "I'll leave the tank in this same spot," Ravi said, before climbing in himself. There hadn't been room for the large vehicle with all eight of them in there.

"After testing it out, of course," Niko added. He turned to go, but Dash reached out for him.

"Thank you again for everything you did to get me here. I feel a hundred times better."

"No problem," Niko said. "Thank you for not bursting into flames when I did it."

Dash raised one eyebrow. "Was that a possibility?"

Niko smiled and shrugged. "Ya never know." He stepped inside and shut the door behind him.

The ground team watched the *Cloud Cat* take off, and then double-checked the maps Chris had loaded onto their MTBs. "The Horn Tree is the tallest, oldest, most sacred tree of the Elfin Forest," Siena said, twisting her arm back and forth to get a clearer view of the small screen. "It says we should do our best to reach it without being spotted and only talk to the two guards posted out front. That must be new info from Chris's update, to help us save time. Supposedly, we should have spotted it easily as we flew in." She looked up from the readout. "Did anyone think to look before we landed?"

The other three shook their heads, then craned their necks to look up at the forest. "They all look the same height from here," Gabriel said.

Siena turned to Piper. "Can your chair go up high enough to scope out the area?"

"I honestly don't know," she said. "Those trees are really high."

"Maybe for a regular person," Gabriel said. "But not for someone who once strapped a gassy robot onto her lap and sailed through outer space."

Piper grinned. "True. Okay, I'll give it a try. As long as the trees don't disrupt the signal between the ground and the chair it should work."

"Do you want company?" Siena asked. "You know, like we did this morning?"

Piper shook her head. "Thanks, but I can only go a few feet off the ground with more than just me."

"Be careful," Dash said. "Come down if it feels too dangerous."

Piper gave him a salute and zoomed straight up until they lost sight of her among the wide branches and large leaves.

The foliage got thicker as Piper flew higher. She slowed down in order to carefully maneuver through the maze of branches. At one point, she couldn't see anything but the green leaves all around her. Just when she thought she'd never reach the top, the closely knit branches started to thin and she broke into a clearing between one tree and another enough that she could see blue sky above.

Piper smiled and pushed her amazing chair to top speed. She brought up her hand to shade her eyes from the glow of the orange suns. She was almost above the trees, where she could get the best view, when—*whoosh!* Piper's chair dropped twenty feet, slamming into a mess of branches. It slid, toppling over so that Piper now hung upside down. She could feel herself sliding along a wide branch, lower and lower. The crackling of leaves and wood sounded, and Piper knew she was about to plummet hundreds of feet to the ground. Her fingers grasped at the joystick, desperate to get the motor restarted.

There was a loud *snap!* and Piper's chair slid rapidly down the broken branch, flipping right side up again. She finally managed to hit the correct button, and her chair suddenly hummed to life, propelling her straight up toward the blue sky. She slowed and hovered just above a solid-looking set of branches. Her heart pounded as she took a couple of deep breaths.

Down on the ground, Siena, Dash, and Gabriel craned their necks looking for any sign of Piper.

"There she is!" Siena shouted, pointing out a golden speck in the air. "That's her hair!" A few very tense moments later, they could see the rest of her, carefully floating down through the leaves. Her face was paler than usual when she reached them.

"It was touchy for a few seconds there," Piper said, peeling off a few stray leaves from her clothes. "The chair must have lost signal strength or something. I was pretty sure I'd be making a new home in the treetops—or falling back down to you, rather than flying!"

She shook out the last of the leaves and said, "So . . . you know how we're supposed to walk backward and whistle when we first approach the elves or they might take our being here as a declaration of war? Yeah, well, it might be too late for that."

"What do you mean?" Gabriel asked.

"A girl in a flying wheelchair is a little hard to miss. If anyone was looking up, they'd have seen me."

"They're supposed to be friendly, though, right?" Dash asked.

Siena nodded. "Chris's records in the library confirmed that. His notes talked a lot about how kind and generous they are with each other. But after the ogres were so awful to them, it makes sense they wouldn't like outsiders."

"Did you find the Horn Tree?" Gabriel asked.

Piper nodded. "And from the top I could see the horn itself. It's inside a room in a sort of tree house about halfway up."

"How far away is it?" Gabriel asked.

"It's in the center of the woods, about a mile deep. If you guys run behind me, we can make it in ten minutes."

"Easy peasy," Gabriel said, slinging his backpack onto his shoulders.

"Famous last words," Siena muttered as she dashed into the woods after the others.

17

The temperature in the forest felt twenty degrees cooler, and the tree cover was so complete that they could only see tiny patches of sky far above. The utter quiet made the crunching of the leaves under their feet sound like thunder. "Can't you guys run more quietly?" Piper called back to them. No one answered. They were too busy avoiding large roots from the massive trees, the occasional fallen log, and the small creatures that darted back and forth across their path. The animals looked like a cross between a rabbit and a mouse, with twitchy noses and fluffy tails. They'd be cute if they weren't slowing down their progress.

After about five minutes dodging mabbits (or *rouses,* Dash couldn't decide what to call them), Dash still felt great. He could leap over the foot-high roots without stumbling, and kept pace with the others. And then suddenly he couldn't. If Siena hadn't pulled him back, he'd have run right into a moss-covered rock the size of a house.

"Hold up," she called to the others.

Dash leaned against the rock, trying to figure out what had just happened. He wasn't short of breath. His legs weren't tired. But his balance was clearly off. He put both hands on the rock to steady himself. "Take deep breaths," Piper demanded.

"It's okay," he said after following her orders. "I feel better." To test it out, he took his hands off the rock and tried walking a few steps in a straight line. "See?"

"Not bad," Gabriel said, leaning up against the rock. The thick moss made it feel soft against his back. "But can you do it while rubbing your belly and patting your head?"

Dash proved that yes, he could, although it took more concentration than he'd admit.

"Nice." Gabriel nodded approvingly.

"Um, Gabriel?" Siena said. "Can you move away from that rock? Like, super fast?"

Gabriel picked up his backpack and walked forward. "Do you want to test my balance too? Because I used to walk to school with a book on my head so—"

"No," she said, grabbing his arm and yanking him toward her. "It's because that rock isn't a rock!"

They all watched with open mouths as the "rock" slowly unfurled two thick arms, lifted a head the size of a car, and stretched its broad moss-covered back—the same back Dash and Gabriel had leaned against! They inched backward as the giant—for clearly that's what it was—slowly began to stand. It must have been at least sixty feet tall, almost as tall as the tops of the trees.

"Uh, that's not an ogre, right?" Gabriel asked. "Because I'm pretty sure Chris didn't say they were a million miles high."

Siena rolled her eyes. "It can't be a million miles high. It isn't even as tall as the trees. And it's clearly not an ogre. Ogres are much smaller than this."

"Then what is it?" Gabriel said.

"Guys, whatever it is, I think it's time to run," Dash said, backing away already.

Before the giant could turn around and spot them, Piper grabbed the others and motioned for them to start running. They took off around the nearest tree, trying to put as much distance between themselves and the giant as possible.

They passed two more of the mossy rocks as they moved deeper into the forest. "Let's let sleeping giants sleep," Gabriel whispered.

No one argued.

A few moments later, they slowed and finally came to a stop to catch their breath. "I think we're okay," Dash said, looking behind them. The giant was easy to spot between trees, and he'd only moved a few feet.

"Guess Chris forgot to tell us there were *giants* here too," Siena said. Dash, Piper, and Gabriel all shrugged. They were used to Chris leaving out key pieces of information despite his insistence otherwise.

Piper took a minute to get her bearings, then said, "Okay, follow me. We're not too far now."

After only a few minutes, Piper stopped short and pointed

a few yards ahead. A rock wall at least ten feet high fanned out in both directions. She hadn't seen that from above. The wall clearly hadn't been well maintained. In some places, half the large rocks had shifted, leaving gaps big enough to crawl through.

They approached it cautiously, bending to look through the holes. The trees on the other side were even wider than the ones behind them. "Didn't Chris say the elves live in the trees?" Dash asked. Siena nodded. "They must be hollow inside." They tried peeking through different gaps, but it was hard to make out any details. Large leaves and thick greenish black moss hung over everything. They couldn't see any doors or windows or smoke from cooking fires. Nothing to suggest life. But at least they also didn't see any giants.

Siena backed away. "Maybe the elves are all gone. It's been a hundred years since Chris was here, right?"

"If that's true," Gabriel said. "It would make our job a lot easier."

"Gabriel Parker!" Piper scolded. "That's not nice. You're talking about a whole species."

Gabriel held up his hand. "Hey, I'm as curious to see an elf as the next guy."

Piper pursed her lips but didn't reply.

"The less time we spend wandering through the village— or whatever this is—the better. Let's wait to climb the wall until we get closer to the Horn Tree."

They turned east and ran around the periphery of the wall,

keeping on the lookout for any movement. After another two minutes, Piper stopped again. "The tree is about a hundred yards past this part of the wall."

Dash went first, testing out a few different spots until he found one that felt steady enough to climb. Piper floated to the top and kept watch. All the practice on the rock wall in the training room paid off, and everyone easily scaled it. The trees were spaced farther apart than on the other side of the wall, and more of the sky peeked through the branches. A huge slab of rock lay in the middle of a clearing, raised a few inches off the ground by other smaller rocks. When they got closer, they saw that what must have once been a meal covered the surface. Wooden plates held the remains of colorful berries and the bones of some kind of meat. Piper hoped it wasn't those cute mabbits (they'd agreed that was the better name), but knew it probably was.

"Okay," Dash said, "I guess the elves are still alive, which is good. But does anyone else think it's creepy that no one's here?"

They all nodded.

"Anyone know what they're supposed to look like?" Dash asked. "Chris didn't describe them."

"None of Chris's records in the library had pictures," Siena said.

"Maybe they're all around us, but invisible!" Gabriel suggested. "Or maybe, like in LOTR, they're totally beautiful and perfect, and looking at them will make you fall instantly in love."

"Not sure that's what happens in the books," Piper pointed out, but Gabriel was on a roll. "Or maybe they're green with pointy ears!" he continued. "And only three inches tall, which explains why this table is so low to the ground!" He fell to his knees and began sifting through the grass, pretending to look for them.

Siena and Piper giggled.

"Let's assume none of those are the right answers," Dash said, trying not to smile. "We'll just have to keep our eyes open for any movement."

"What if no one's at the tree when we get there?" Siena asked.

"We're about to find out," Piper said, pointing to a nearby tree that was so tall, no one could see the top of it. They couldn't see any guards either. They spread out to search the immediate area.

The Horn Tree was so wide that it took a few minutes before they circled it and met back up again. Except for the mabbits, nothing moved in the woods at all.

"Wherever they are," Piper said, "they must not care about guarding the horn anymore. After all this time, they've probably gotten so used to not being attacked by the ogres that they don't see the point of posting guards."

"Or maybe they don't even remember what the horn does," Siena suggested. "Or even that it's there at all."

"Pretty sure they remember," Gabriel said. In his search for a doorway into the tree, he had pushed aside some of the huge leaves and exposed a large part of the tree trunk. Rather than the gray bark that they could see peeking out from the other trees, this portion of the tree was white and smooth. Drawings covered most of the space. The image in the center—the one surrounded by yellow and pink flowers—was everyone's favorite alien.

"That guy sure gets around," Gabriel said with an approving whistle. "They even captured his bubbly personality." Gabriel stepped next to the drawing, imitating Chris's expression, which was really just showing no emotion at all.

Piper and Siena rolled their eyes. Dash stepped closer to inspect the rest of the drawings. The whole scene clearly depicted the story of Chris making the horn and using it to put the ogres to sleep. The ogres were nasty-looking creatures with beady black eyes, long hooked noses, and arms that hung longer than they should. Nowhere in the pictures did they see anything that resembled elves, though.

"Okay," Dash said, "so the elves know the story. Then where are they?"

"That depends," an unfamiliar female voice rang out from behind them, "on who's asking and what they want."

18

The ground team would have turned around faster had there not been the sharp ends of spears jabbing not so gently into their shoulders. Dash cleared his throat and held up his hands. "We come in peace," he said, cringing at how lame that sounded. "We're friends of Chris." He motioned with his head at the picture on the tree. "You know, *that* guy." The point of the spear pressed a little more harshly into his back when his head moved, so he froze again.

"You have interrupted Feast Day," a deeper voice accused. "You have trespassed on our village while we bathed in the sea in celebration of a hundred years of peace. And now you stand before our most sacred tree and mock us? Explain yourselves!"

"Please," Piper asked in her sweetest voice. "We really are friendly and mean no harm. Can we please turn around and talk?"

After a long moment of silence, the male voice answered. "Power down your weapon first."

"Um, what weapon?" Piper asked, holding out her empty hands.

"The one you sit upon."

"Oh, this," Piper said, still keeping her voice light. "It's not a weapon. I use it to get around. My legs don't work."

The voices conferred with each other in a language the kids couldn't understand. Finally, the spears pulled back. The four of them turned around slowly, rubbing their necks where the points had dug in. Gabriel gasped. "OMG, I was right!"

Two elves stood before them, towels draped over their shoulders. Gabriel thought they looked like regular Earthly teenagers back from a day at the beach except for a few very distinct differences. Their ears were indeed pointy—not like Spock on *Star Trek* pointy, but the tops definitely weren't round. And second, these two would have been on the covers of magazines back home. Or been, like, pop stars. Pimple-free green(ish) skin, long flowing black hair, bright gold eyes. He couldn't help gaping at them and didn't think he could have spoken to save his life.

Dash cleared his throat, doing an only slightly better job of not staring. If the elves didn't have those spears, they wouldn't look very scary at all. "Um, I'm Dash, and this is Piper, Siena, and the one with his mouth hanging open is Gabriel. We have come to speak with the horn guards."

"We are the horn guards," the male replied, turning his head briefly to glare at Gabriel, who was too busy staring at the female elf to notice. "I am Tumar, and this is my cousin Lythe. Why have you come here?"

"Chris sent us," Dash said. "You know, alien guy, brown hair, kind of serious all the time?"

"And very handsome," Piper added.

Dash raised an eyebrow at her. She smiled and shrugged. Siena giggled.

"We know of no one by that name," Tumar claimed.

Dash pointed at the tree again. "His picture's right there. With all the colorful flowers around it?"

The elves glanced at the tree. "Oh!" Lythe said, her face lighting up. "You mean Chrysanthemum?"

"Chrysanthemum?" Piper repeated. "Like the flower?"

The elves nodded. "That was his name," Lythe said. "There's a famous song about him."

"I'd like to hear that sometime," Piper said, a mischievous gleam in her eye.

Dash had to force aside how easy it would be to tease Chris about this name when they returned to the ship. "Well," he said, "we just know him as Chris. And he said you were aware that one day he would return to sound the horn and awaken the ogres." Dash paused and tried to sound as commanding as possible when he said, "That day has come."

The elves' faces darkened, and their hands tightened around their spears. Dash quickly added, "It would only be temporary, like for one day, and then we'd sound the horn again and put them back to sleep forever."

Siena made a slight sound of dissent, which Dash covered up by pretending to cough.

"Why would we do this?" Lythe asked. Gabriel thought her

voice sounded like the wind chimes on his grandmother's front porch. He loved those wind chimes.

When Dash explained how Earth was almost out of power and they needed this last ingredient to save their world, Tumar laughed. It wasn't a cruel laugh, more a disbelieving one. "You come here on Feast Day, want us to end a hundred years of peace, then let a dragon burn down one of our trees? That is an absurd request."

Unable to deny that it really did sound crazy, Dash said, "Guess our timing isn't great, but we wouldn't ask if it wasn't so important. Like I said, our whole planet is in danger. Just a bit of dragon cinder is all we're asking."

Tumar and Lythe exchanged a look, and then a nod. Dash breathed a sigh of relief. They were over the first hurdle. But the elves didn't move toward the tree. Dash glanced up. The suns were quickly moving across the sky. They needed to get the ogres on the move before dark. "I'm sorry to have to rush this," he said, "and you two seem like really lovely people—I mean, elves—and we'd love to hang out and get to know each other better, but we're really pressed for time. Can you bring us to the horn now?"

When they still didn't move, it became evident they were never going to. Guess that nod was an agreement *not* to help them. Piper swiveled her chair to face them directly. "You may not like it now, but you *did* make a deal with Chris. You were to awaken the ogres one last time, and in return, he would take the horn far from here so you'd never have to worry about them again. You wouldn't have had that century of peace without him. You owe him this."

"Lythe and I made no such deal with anyone," Tumar said.

Lythe leaned closer to her cousin. "But maybe our grandparents did?"

"*Maybe* they did?" Dash repeated. "Isn't that why you're guarding the horn? Because someday you knew we'd be back?"

"We guard it because our family has always guarded it," Lythe explained.

Dash was beginning to get an uneasy feeling. Had Chris lied to them about having a deal? Or did the elves truly not know of the agreement?

Tumar stomped his foot. "If our grandparents made that deal, then they were desperate and would say anything to get the ogres to leave us alone. Their generation had never known peace before Chrysanthemum arrived. But *we* have. We are not willing to give it up for some deal made a hundred years ago, if it was made at all."

"That's not good sportsmanship!" Piper told the elves, crossing her arms. Siena eyed the fallen branches nearby. One of them would definitely make a serviceable sword. She was pretty sure she could take 'em both in a fight if she had to.

Dash turned to Gabriel. "Any ideas here? You seem to be the expert on elves."

Gabriel forced himself to turn away from Lythe to focus on Dash. Then he grinned and began to whistle. It took a second before the others realized why. Being met with spears had made them forget the customary greeting! It was too late to approach them backward, but they could still whistle. Dash joined in, followed by the girls.

It was not a pretty sound. The elves' eyes widened, and they winced. "What are you doing?" Lythe asked, putting her hands over her ears.

They stopped, except for Gabriel, who was clearly enjoying himself. He may not be as good as Ravi, but he could carry a decent tune. He whistled a few more bars of "Amazing Grace," and then bowed deeply. Siena clapped.

Lythe's face softened a bit, and she lowered her spear. Tumar hesitated, then did the same. "Look, this isn't easy for us," he said. "We'd help if we could."

"Then take us to your leader," Dash said, cringing again. That was almost as bad as *we come in peace*!

"I assure you, King Urelio will tell you the same thing," Tumar said.

Lythe motioned her cousin over and said something else in their elfin language. "I will bring the king here instead," Tumar announced. "He is still at the sea and would not want a stranger at the ceremony."

"Fine," Dash said. Tumar gave Lythe instructions on guarding them and then darted off so quickly he looked like a greenish blur.

They stood around awkwardly. Gabriel began peppering Lythe with questions. How old was she? What was life like in their village? What did elves do for fun? Dash was about to tell him to give her a break, but realized Gabriel was doing an excellent job of distracting her. Piper saw it too. The two of them inched closer together until Piper was close enough to whisper into Dash's ear. "The horn is halfway up the tree, directly over Chris's head. I mean, over the drawing of Chris's head."

Dash pretended to stretch, and looked up. He could spot the glint of the white horn between the leaves. He whispered back out of the corner of his mouth. "If the king comes and refuses to honor the deal, we'll be escorted out of here. This might be our only chance."

Piper nodded grimly.

"Did I ever mention I was a pitcher for my second-grade pee-wee baseball team?" Dash said.

She shook her head.

"Yup. My fastball clocked in at around twenty miles per hour."

"That doesn't sound very fast," she said.

"I was seven. What I lacked in speed I made up for in accuracy." He squinted up at the window. "I think I can make it."

Siena followed their gaze and quickly figured out what they were talking about. Her mouth formed a tight line, but she gave them a begrudging nod of approval. Then she walked over to Lythe and started talking hair care. Yes, hair care. Dash had never heard Siena say anything remotely girly before, and now she was comparing the difficulties of maintaining the shine and fullness of her long, dark hair in this humid environment and did Lythe have any tips on how she kept hers so smooth? Clearly flattered, the elf girl was only too happy to explain how she applied the perfect mixture of seaweed, pollen, and morning dew. Gabriel seemed fascinated by the conversation.

As they talked, Dash bent down and pretended to tie his boot while his eyes scanned the ground for the perfect stone. Most of them were too large, and he was afraid he wouldn't get it high enough if it was too heavy. He would only have one chance.

He spotted a stone near Gabriel's foot that looked good. He

inched over, pretending to be interested in their conversation. This proved painful, as the girls were now talking skin care. Lythe had pulled a leaf off a nearby tree and was showing Siena the thin film of liquid you get when you scrape the underside with your fingernail. "It makes an excellent moisturizer," she said in her singsong voice. "See?" the elf girl began rubbing the leaf on the back of Siena's hand.

"Ooh, soft," Siena said.

"Look at that cool bug!" Dash exclaimed, crouching down and yanking Gabriel down with him.

"Go on the other side of Lythe so she has to turn around to face you," Dash hissed as he palmed the stone. "I need ten seconds." He pulled Gabriel back to his feet before he could ask any questions. Gabriel did as he was told, and Lythe turned her body away from the Horn Tree. Dash stepped back, and Piper positioned herself between him and the others.

Knowing he couldn't afford to hesitate, Dash raised his arm and threw the stone at the tiny sliver of the horn that he could see. He heard the leaves rustle as it sailed through the branches. The rock hit the horn squarely, and Dash held his breath as it teetered before finally tipping completely over and falling straight out of the opening in the tree.

Dash paused for just a second before racing to stand under the falling horn. It was larger than he'd imagined, and he had to catch it cradle-style when it almost reached the ground. The horn was so heavy, it knocked Dash on his back when he caught it.

Lythe stopped midsentence, hearing the noise behind her. She stopped to turn, and just when Dash thought he was caught, Gabriel caught Lythe's hand. With a terrified look on his face,

Gabriel pulled the elf close and, just like he'd seen in the movies, tipped Lythe back and tried to deliver the most romantic line he'd ever heard. Instead, he said, "Live long and prosper."

Dash gaped at Gabriel and Lythe for a moment before Piper whisper-shouted, "Do it!" Returning to the task at hand, Dash rushed to stand up. He lifted the great horn to his mouth. He took a deep breath and blew into the mouthpiece of the horn as hard he could and . . .

Nothing happened.

Dash lowered the horn to inspect it. Maybe there was something clogging it?

Lythe suddenly shoved Gabriel away and turned to Dash. "No!" she shouted.

"Guess you're not a *Star Trek* fan . . . ," Gabriel said, blushing.

Lythe advanced toward Dash and tried to snatch the horn out of his arms. Piper flew between them, blocking Lythe's reach.

"Why did you do that?" Lythe cried.

"I didn't do anything," Dash insisted.

"You sounded the horn!"

Dash, Piper, and Siena exchanged puzzled glances. How did she know? They hadn't heard anything.

"Maybe the sound resonates on some higher frequency," Piper suggested. "Like it's so high-pitched only dogs can hear it. Dogs and ogres, that is."

Lythe threw her head back and howled.

Piper slid down in her chair. "Um, we might want to run."

19

Ten miles to the east, in a deep, dark, moldy cave, one hundred ogres yawned, stretched, and sat up. In single file, they staggered out onto the rocky shores of the Dargon coast, squinting and bumping into each other. They grunted as they saw each other's extra-long nose hair, felt their stiff bones, and realized something was very, very wrong.

On the beach now, the ogres grunted and yanked at their nose hair until it tore right out. They threw it on the sand in disgust and took long, deep breaths through their tunnel-like nostrils. They spread out on the shore and sniffed in all directions. The scents that filled their noses were familiar— the sea air, the fresh soil of the nearby woods, the sickly-sweet smell of the elves, the overripe-cheese aroma of giants, and something . . . new. They sniffed harder, turning this way and that, trying to identify this new scent on the wind. It did not pose a threat, they could tell that, but the ogres liked to be in charge of their environment at all times.

They sniffed until one of the ogres turned to face the northern mountain peaks and the others followed. At once, their lips spread wide, revealing rows of broken yellow teeth. This was the closest the ogres came to smiling. The new scent forgotten, they filled their lungs with the ashy, sharp, smoky smell of fire. Their favorite smell of all. The smell of dragons.

The ogres were hungry. They were angry. Somehow the elves had trapped them in that cave for a long, long time. It was time to get the dragons and seek revenge.

On board the *Cloud Leopard,* Ravi and Niko were just returning from leaving the tank on the planet. They were following a long list that Chris had given them on how to prepare the ship to handle the Source. The power surge would be so enormous, Chris was worried it would fry the electronic components on the ship. He had all available hands—human and ZRK—reinforcing the weak links with a special surge protector he'd cobbled together. Chris himself was spending all his time down in the *Cloud Kitten.*

Ravi checked his MTB for the time. By now, the elves should have sounded the horn and awakened the ogres. The ground crew was no doubt working with the elves to help steer the ogres away from the Elfin Forest.

What was actually happening on the planet below was a little different. Gabriel, Dash, and Siena were standing inside the Horn Tree, about halfway up. Piper hovered outside the window, since the stairs inside were too narrow for her to navigate. If they weren't flanked on both sides by elves with spears, Gabriel would totally enjoy what was hands down the coolest tree house he had ever been in. Oil lanterns glowing red, then yellow, then blue, lit their way up a winding wooden staircase, where every stair had been stained a different color. Circular beds hung from vines, and zip lines zigzagged all the way from the top to the floor. Gabriel itched to try them.

The leader of the elves—a robed man with a silver beard who looked exactly how Gabriel thought a king of the elves *should* look—was currently screaming at Dash for having the nerve, the gall, the sheer *hubris* to sound the horn without permission.

Gabriel was indeed using his skills of charm and sincerity, and he was hoping these traits would help them now. While Dash bore the brunt of the king's fury, Gabriel was doing his best to convince Lythe to keep the leader from re-sounding the horn. "Please tell them how important this is," he begged her in as loud a whisper as he dared. "They wouldn't have made you the horn guard if they didn't trust your judgment."

Lythe scoffed. "Look where my judgment got me!" she whispered back. "I'm the last person they'll listen to now."

"I don't think so," he insisted. "Guarding the horn is in your blood. Yours and Tumar's. They *have* to listen to you."

Lythe let his words play in her head. She had to admit this alien—the first she'd ever met—was growing on her. She liked the dark-haired girl too. She was a good listener. Usually no one asked her for tips on anything. Even though the boy with the messy hair had gone behind her back to sound the horn, for some reason she wanted to trust them. She could tell they weren't lying about the agreement—somehow she just knew they were telling the truth.

This boy who called himself Gabriel was right—the legend of the horn was in her blood.

She squeezed her eyes shut so she wouldn't see his pleading gaze. She just wished she had some proof! A few seconds later, her eyes flew open. She *did* have proof! She glanced at Tumar. Had he started to believe them too? She didn't have time to find out.

"Please, my lord," she said, bowing her head slightly. "As one of those entrusted with the job of guarding the horn, I ask that you hear my words."

The king turned to her. An expression of annoyance flitted across his green face. She looked to the boy Gabriel for support. He gave her a nod, and his eyes were warm. She took a breath. "I believe these strangers are telling the truth. The tree itself tells the story."

"What do you mean by those words?" the king asked.

She took another breath. "Outside, sir. The old paintings. They have been covered by branches and vines for many years. There is a painting of the horn being lifted onto a ship. A ship that flies! One just like the one we saw in the sky only this morning. This must mean that their story is true. We must help them, and then they will help us one final time and take the horn far away forever."

The king lowered his spear. The tips of his pointy ears twitched. He looked at Lythe for what felt like an eternity before slowly nodding. "If this proves true," the king said, "you shall have your one day. I will place guards at the four corners of the Elfin Forest to protect our sacred trees from the ogres, but if we cannot keep them away, I will sound that horn."

Dash wanted to remind him that part of the deal would require the elves to lose at least one sacred tree, but decided it would be wiser to hold that back for now and let the king focus on the ogre problem. So he simply said, "Thank you, sir. One day is all we ask." He didn't add that one day was all he had.

"And I demand to see Chrysanthemum for myself," the king added. "I will need to verify you are acting under his orders."

Dash was about to tell him that was impossible due to the signal being blocked by the sound waves of the horn, when he realized that wasn't true anymore. He turned over his wrist and typed in a few numbers, hoping Chris was wearing his own MTB. He noticed the elves were tightening their holds on their spears.

Dash let out a long sigh of relief when Chris's face popped up on the small screen. A splotch of oil streaked across Chris's cheek, and he looked tired. "Chris!" Dash said hurriedly. "We sounded the horn, but the king wants to be sure we really came with you before he helps us. Can you tell him?"

"They let you sound the horn?" Chris asked, squinting up at him.

Dash glanced at his friends before answering. "Well, not so much *let* us, exactly, but they did say they'd help if you tell them—"

"Yes," Chris interrupted. "These children are with me. Thank you for letting them continue their very important mission."

Gabriel and Siena both bristled at being called children. The elves in the room murmured excitedly. Here was the famous Chrysanthemum!

"And in return you will take the horn with you?" the king asked Chris, although it sounded more like a command than a question.

"Yes, yes," Chris promised.

"How will you—"

But Chris interrupted again. "We will take care of it. I must go." Dash's screen turned dark.

The king sputtered for a few seconds, clearly not used to being dismissed.

"Um, he's really busy with ship stuff," Siena said, trying to smooth things over.

"You have one day," the king snapped, "not a second more. Lythe! Tumar!" The two horn guards snapped to attention. "Since you seem to think we can trust these strangers, you will accompany them. And this time I expect you will keep a closer eye on them, yes?" Without another word, he stormed off down the stairs, waving for the other elves to follow him. Tumar and Lythe stayed behind. Gabriel, Siena, and Dash went to the window to join Piper and plan their next move.

"I feel a little bad saying this," Piper said when they were alone, "but did Chris seem unusually rude to the king just now?"

"Totally," Siena said.

"Dash?" Siena said, waving her hands in front of his face to get his attention. He hadn't looked up from his arm since the call. "Dash? Didn't you think Chris was kind of obnoxious?"

Dash shook his head. When he finally looked up, his face had gone pale, even paler than usual. When he spoke, his tone was grim.

"That wasn't Chris."

20

The storehouse of axes and shields were right where the ogres had left them, tucked underneath an outcrop of rocks by the shoreline. The site was only visible when the suns set and cast a certain light on the rocks, showing the ogres where their sacred stash was kept, ensuring that the elves would never find their stores. The ogres did not know exactly how much time had passed, for the forest and the shore and the mountain peaks they used to call home looked the same as they remembered. Only the rust on the locks and the warping of the door hinted at the years. The weapons themselves—having been treated with grease made from worm guts and the ogres' own saliva—remained shiny and sharp.

Now armed, the ogres made their plan. Half wanted to attack the elves right away, to chop at their precious tree branches. The elves would chase them with their swords and spears, but they would get some good swings in first. The other half of the ogres

wanted to climb the mountain and awaken the dragons. While it would be satisfying to see tree limbs fall, it would be *glorious* to watch the trees burn.

It was decided that half the ogres would ascend the mountain. Once at home on the high, windy peaks, they would do as they'd always done—prod and taunt the ferocious winged beasts until down they flew, breathing their fiery anger upon the elves' village.

The other half of the ogres would remain below to generally raise a ruckus and start trouble.

Before going their separate ways, the two halves faced each other in long, even rows. They stuck out their axes, clanged them together, grunted, and smacked foreheads.

They were ready.

The ground crew along with Lythe and Tumar raced back through the woods. Dash was trying to contact the ship, but no one was answering. Fighting off his rising panic, he said, "We have to focus on our mission here. Colin can't take the ship anywhere without us. There's no way to get the ship back in Gamma." He needed the crew to believe everything on the *Cloud Leopard* was fine. Even if he didn't believe it himself.

"Wait," Tumar said, grabbing Dash's arm. The group stopped running, panting to catch their breath. "If you have a plan, we need to know what it is. King Urelio will not—"

"King Urelio only gave us one day to complete this mission," Dash interrupted. "I promise you, I will tell you our plan, but we have little time and need to keep moving."

Dash turned to start running again, but Tumar thrust his spear in Dash's face. "We're not going anywhere until Lythe and I know the plan."

Following Tumar's cue, Lythe lifted her spear as well, if only halfheartedly.

Dash glared at Tumar. This was just what they needed: unhelpful elves. "The plan is to complete our mission as quickly as possible. And that means running. Now."

"Look," Gabriel said, stepping forward and nearly tripping over a large tree root. "Dash is right—we need to keep moving. What if the ogres woke up, realized they haven't eaten in a hundred years, and decided to raid your village first? The sooner we get this plan in action, the sooner we can save all of you from ever having to deal with the ogres again."

Tumar and Dash continued to glare at one another until Lythe laid her hand gently on Tumar's arm. "I think we need to go along for now. I trust them," she said.

Tumar reluctantly lowered his spear. "Well, I don't," he said. "But I'll trust your judgment. For now. We may continue, but you will tell us of your plan the instant we arrive at this . . . flying ship."

Dash nodded. "Actually," he said as he turned to run, "we're not going to our ship."

The rest of the ground crew followed him. Tumar and Lythe easily kept pace. "Then how will you get all the way to the mountain in less than a day?" Lythe asked.

Dash shielded his eyes from the glare of the sun, which was

slipping lower into the sky every minute. "With *that*," he replied, pointing at the tank that was now sitting at the landing spot. "Our new best friend."

Up in the *Cloud Leopard,* the situation was bleak. Colin, who had pretended to be Chris until now, had his glasses back on and was feeling pretty proud of himself. He was finally in control of the ship and things would be done *his* way.

"What have you done to Chris?" Ravi asked, glaring at Colin from about four inches away from his face. They were gathered below the engine room, where Chris lay on the floor of the *Cloud Kitten,* unconscious. Rocket was whimpering beside him, his paws on Chris's leg. Carly was the only one missing. Without their MTBs, they didn't know where she was. She must have taken hers off, or else Colin would have rounded her up too.

"You better step back, little boy," Colin warned.

"Who you calling little?" Ravi said, standing straighter. He was only a few inches shorter than Colin.

Niko—who was smaller than the rest of the crew by a good six inches and was used to being called little—pulled on Ravi's arm, but Ravi didn't budge. You couldn't grow up in a family as big as Ravi's and not stand up for yourself. True, usually his approach to confrontation was usually to defuse the situation by telling a joke, but he knew that wouldn't work here. Plus, he was too angry to joke now.

"I said, step back!" Colin growled.

"Or what?" Anna asked, stepping up alongside Ravi.

"Or I'll knock you out like I did Chris," Colin said with a sneer. They didn't know that technically he couldn't do that. Only Chris was allergic to the Walla-nika plant he'd discovered in Chris's room.

For the first time on the entire voyage, Anna was speechless. Colin was mean and had done some pretty rotten things but never anything so violent. She'd never been truly scared of him until now.

The truth was that Colin couldn't hurt them. He needed them in order to make the *Cloud Kitten* (how he hated that ridiculous name!) fly on its own.

So far, Colin had learned a lot about this alien ship. The main engines of the *Cloud Leopard* and the *Cloud Kitten* were still linked, but many features now worked independently. Soon the *Cloud Kitten* would be able to break free. Colin would still need the Source to power it, though; there was no getting around that. And that meant these kids still served a purpose, both on board and on the planet.

"You have jobs to do," Colin boomed. His voice was enough to make Anna and Ravi take a step backward. "Now go finish them."

"Give us our Mobile Tech Bands back," Anna demanded. "We can't do our jobs without being able to communicate with each other. And the ground crew might need us. Judging from how eagerly you asked the elves if the horn had been sounded, you want to get back to Earth now as much as we do." As soon as she said it, though, a trickle of doubt entered her mind. *Did* he want to go back? Or did he have some other plan they weren't aware of?

Colin pushed the MTBs deeper into his pockets. "You will manage without these. If the ground crew needs anything, I will respond."

"He better be okay," Anna said, gesturing back at Chris. "He's the only one who knows how to get us home."

Ignoring her remark, Colin said, "I don't want to see the three of you until the ground crew returns. Then everyone will report to me immediately."

When they got outside the previously hidden room, Niko said, "He totally doesn't think Carly's on the ship. Wouldn't he have tracked her MTB, like he tracked ours? It should be picking up her vital stats, heart rate, breathing, like always."

Ravi felt a shiver of fear. "Last I saw her she was working on the Element Fuser. She's okay, right?"

"Let's go find out," Anna said, running toward the portal.

21

In the engine room, the tank had looked pretty impressive and foreboding—much larger than the watercraft they'd used on Aqua Gen or the Streak they'd driven on Tundra. But in comparison to the huge trees, the tank looked like a small metal box that a giant could crush in his fist like a dry autumn leaf.

Gabriel climbed in first and gave a long whistle. "This place is swanky!"

The inside of the tank looked more like a luxury car than a metal war machine. Padded bench seats ran the length of the tank on either side, and cots that pulled down from the walls created instant bunk beds. There were pillows, blankets, and even a collection of plush animals.

"The ZRKs must have been bored on the long ride in Gamma," Piper said. Lythe and Tumar stepped in tentatively after her.

"But does it actually move?" Siena asked, bringing up the rear with Dash.

"Let's see what this bad boy can do," Gabriel said. He turned the large yellow key one notch to the right, and the engine purred to life. Gabriel frowned. He'd expected the loud grinding of gears, the churning of rubber as the wheels kicked up dirt, but the tank moved along smoothly, almost soundlessly. Oh well, at least they were moving.

Speed proved not to be one of the tank's strengths. "I think we can walk faster than this," Gabriel grumbled. Siena settled in the back of the tank. Tumar and Lythe perched uneasily together on the seat next to Gabriel.

Piper swung out of her chair and slid over next to Dash, who was trying to keep his breathing even so the others wouldn't worry. They both started—and stopped—to say something about the Colin situation. After a short silence, which they spent staring out the closest window, Piper said, "Doesn't it seem like the mountain is getting farther away, rather than nearer?"

Dash nodded. It really did seem that way. "The way the valley dips down makes it hard for our eyes to judge the distance."

Piper smiled.

"What's so funny?" Dash asked.

"I was really just making conversation," she said.

"Oh. Right." They watched the scenery go by again until the motion of the tank lulled them both to sleep.

Dash's eyes snapped open when a stuffed pink octopus landed on his chest with a thump. "Wake up, fearless leader," Gabriel said from above him. "We've arrived at the base of the mountain. Lythe is out scouting for us." He gave an annoyed look at Tumar, who sat rigid in his seat, holding his spear across his lap.

Dash no longer felt the motion of the wheels beneath him and scrambled to his feet. Piper was already back in her chair. "Did you see the ogres?"

Gabriel nodded. "The good news is the plan is moving forward. The ogres are scaling the mountain right now."

"And the bad news?" Dash asked.

"They're only a quarter of the way up. And they may have stopped for the night because it doesn't look like they're going any higher."

Dash groaned. "We're way behind schedule, then. Anything we can do to make them climb faster?"

As the one who knew the most about the ogres, Siena shook her head. "According to my research, we're unable to communicate with them. They have a very primitive language of grunts and snorts. Chris wasn't able to replicate it for our translator device."

Dash took a deep breath. "Okay. The ZRKs built us this tank to use as shelter. We'll be safe here for the night. Hopefully by dawn they'll have started climbing again. If not, confronting them sounds like our only option. We'll make them understand us."

"I'll try calling the ship again," Gabriel said, already typing on his arm band. He opened a channel to all four of the remaining crew members. "Hi!" Carly said cheerfully. "How's it going down there?"

They all grabbed at Gabriel's arm to answer, but before anyone could get a word out, they heard what sounded like heavy footfalls, and then Anna shouted, "Hang up, hang up! Right now!"

The line went dead.

"What just happened?" Gabriel asked. The ground crew stared at each other.

"Do . . . do you think Anna and Colin are working together?" Siena asked, feeling bad for even thinking it, but clearly Anna's behavior in the past proved she was willing to betray her friends. Maybe she would again.

Dash sank back down onto his sleeping bag. Was he a fool for thinking that Anna could have changed? "I don't want to believe that. I'm sure there's some other explanation."

Silence fell as they tried to think of one. A loud rapping on the side of the tank startled all of them.

Tumar rolled his eyes. "It is only Lythe," he said.

Dash unlatched the front door, then inched it open slowly.

Lythe stood outside, her golden eyes glinting with the reflected light of Dargon's three moons. She held up a basket in each hand. "Hungry?"

"Why'd you make me hang up?" Carly demanded. She was surrounded by her crewmates on all sides. They had pushed her into the narrow storage closet built into the hull beside the Element Fuser. It was cramped, especially with the robots (and her guitar). Carly tried to move her elbow so she could reach her wrist, but Anna's shoulder was in the way. "I need to call Gabriel back," Carly said, twisting so she could pull her arms in closer to her body. "What if the ground team's in trouble and they need us?"

Ravi grabbed for her arm. "Wait. Let us explain."

She raised her eyebrows. "Explain what? That you guys are being total weirdos?"

"Carly, listen," Anna pleaded. "Colin tricked Chris. I mean *really* tricked him. I don't know what he did, but Chris is passed out on the floor of the *Cloud Kitten*. And Colin's taken over the ship. Forget the ground crew. *We're* in big trouble."

STEAM began to sputter angrily. SUMI jumped and hopped but couldn't move very much in the tight space. TULIP just whimpered.

Carly's eyes were wide. "How do you know all this?"

"So you didn't see his conversation with Dash?" Anna asked.

Carly shook her head.

"Colin tracked the rest of us down from our MTB signals," she said, "which is why we didn't want you to use yours. He seems to have forgotten about you." Anna looked around the space. "Have you been working back here all afternoon?"

Carly nodded. "Gabriel's call was the first communication I've gotten today."

"The fuser must be blocking your signal," Ravi said, "or at least severely lowering its strength. Otherwise Colin would have found you too. You should turn yours off, just in case."

Reluctantly, Carly switched her MTB off. She noticed the others didn't have theirs at all. "What did Dash talk to Colin about?"

"The elves needed proof that Dash and the others were really with Chris before agreeing to help them," Niko said. "Colin pretended to be Chris!"

"We need to warn them!" Carly said.

"I think they already know," Ravi replied. "Without his glasses, he may look like Chris, and he definitely fooled the elves. But Dash is smart. He'd have seen right through it."

"Maybe so," Carly said, "but we still need to find out why they called."

"STEAM," Anna called, twisting her head around to look for him. "Any ideas on how to contact the ground crew without Colin picking up the signal? I'm sure he's monitoring the whole ship."

At first, STEAM seemed surprised that she'd spoken to him. It was a rare occurrence. But after a few seconds of calculations, he replied, "Yes."

She waited, then forced herself to hold back her annoyance and asked, "Are you gonna tell us how?"

STEAM pointed at SUMI, who hopped and chirped and proudly said, *"Me."*

22

"**That was the** best strawberry I've ever eaten," Piper declared, wiping the pink juice from her chin with her arm. "Thank you."

"You're welcome," Lythe said, beaming. "I am glad you enjoyed the food."

"Well, I didn't like it at all," Gabriel said through a mouthful of food as he speared his eighth berry with his fork.

Lythe's face fell. "Oh . . . I'm sorry. It was just all I could find this close to the mountain."

Gabriel lowered his fork. "No, *I'm* sorry. I was kidding."

Lythe shook her head. "I don't know what that means."

So Gabriel spent the next ten minutes trying to make her laugh with riddles, puns, and knock-knock jokes. Piper, Siena, and Dash groaned louder with each one. Lythe and Tumar mostly looked confused. They did both seem to like the "orange you glad I didn't say banana" knock-knock joke, though. Or at least they made sounds with their throats that could almost be interpreted as laughter. At least Tumar seemed to be lightening up a little.

"Forgive me for bringing down the party," Dash said to their guests, "but would you happen to know how we could get the ogres to move faster up the mountain?"

The cousins shared a look and shook their heads. "In the days before the Great Peace, the fact that the ogres are so slow to climb was helpful to our people," Tumar said. "Once we saw them ascending the mountain, we knew we had a few days to get to safety, to water down the trees, to try to protect our village as well as we could."

"Did you say *days*?" Dash asked. "As in more than one day?"

The elves nodded. "The mountain peaks are higher than they appear."

"We've noticed that," Piper said, frowning. Then she asked, "How do the ogres track down the dragons, anyway?"

"The dragons have a natural camouflage that helps them blend into the rocks, so finding them by sight is nearly impossible," Lythe explained.

"They give off some kind of smell when they sleep," Tumar said. "It's so faint that we can't pick it up, but the ogres can. With noses that big, I suppose they can smell anything. It leads them straight to the dragons' dens."

"Chris told us humans can't smell the dragons either," Gabriel said. His MTB crackled to life and startled him.

"Hi, Gabriel? Can anyone hear me?" Carly's voice came through the crackling.

"We can hear you!" Gabriel said eagerly, lifting his arm. "I can't see you on the screen, though."

"I'm not using my MTB," Carly said quickly. "I'm coming through SUMI. On that channel you made to contact Piper on the *Light Blade*."

"Oh!" Gabriel said. "Cool."

Dash leaned over. "Carly! Are you guys okay? Why was Colin pretending to be Chris? Is Chris okay? And where's Anna?"

"What do you mean *where's Anna?*" Anna asked. "I'm here taking care of things while you're—"

"We're fine," Carly interrupted. "Well, mostly. Colin knocked Chris unconscious." The ground crew exchanged uneasy glances. "But don't worry about us," Carly continued. "Anna and I have come up with a plan."

Dash raised an eyebrow. Carly sounded normal enough, and if Carly and Anna were working together, then maybe Anna wasn't helping Colin. Maybe Dash had been wrong to doubt her.

"What's happening down there?" asked Carly.

Gabriel told them about the ogres climbing too slow, and about their conversation with Lythe and Tumar. Well, he mostly talked about Lythe.

"Hang on a second," Carly said, distracted. The ground team could hear voices talking hurriedly, with STEAM and SUMI chiming in. Then Anna's voice came through. "Dash! Carly and I think we could synthesize the smell in the lab. Then we could program the *Cloud Cat*'s sensors to recognize the chemical signatures, fly down there, and scare us up some dragons! We would need the elves' help, though."

Lythe and Tumar looked at each other. It was clear from their puzzled expressions that they didn't know what Anna was talking about.

"Basically they want to know if you have anything that might have the dragons' scent on it," Gabriel explained. "Then they can try to imitate it so our smaller ship can find it."

"You mean the flying machine from the painting on the Horn Tree?" Tumar said, his eyes brightening. "Would we be able to see it?"

Dash and Gabriel exchanged glances. Maybe this was how they convinced Tumar to help them. Dash nodded. "Not only see it," Gabriel said, "but you guys can fly in it!"

Tumar jumped up. "I know where I can find some dragon cinder nearby. Might that work?"

More voices on the other end. Anna came back on. "STEAM says if you use your Mobile Tech Band to analyze an object the dragon left its scent on, that could work. You could then send us the data, and we'll make it up here. We can't take a chance on coming down tonight and having Colin catch us."

"We'll do our best," Gabriel promised. "Too bad the Element Fuser needs fresh ash or we'd be all set," he said as the connection broke off. "So where are we headed?" he asked the elves as he prepared to start the tank's engines.

Tumar shook his head. "You cannot go. If you show up at another of our sacred sites, and King Urelio discovers it, he will sound the horn for certain."

"We will get the item for you," Lythe said, standing up to join her cousin. "We will return before the second moon sets to the north." They gathered their cloaks and dashed out the door.

"Wait, when's that?" Gabriel called after them. But they were already gone.

Back on the *Cloud Leopard* several hours later, SUMI hopped over to Anna and Carly, who were busy programming. Their work would have gone faster if they weren't looking over their shoulders for Colin the whole time.

"I have the data," SUMI squeaked. "Will now initiate printing." SUMI lifted her arm, and a long strip of paper slid out from a slot Carly had never noticed before in the robot's armpit. "Thanks, SUMI," she said, studying the printout. She handed it to Anna. "What do you think?"

"I think we have the recipe for dragon cinder."

"Do you think you can separate the part of the dragon cinder that came from the dragon, and the part that came from the tree?"

Anna shook her head. "I don't think I can do it. But I think *we* can." Working together, it took another hour before they were confident that they'd succeeded. All that was left was to use the chemicals in the lab to create a gas out of the equation they'd come up with. Fortunately, the computer did most of the hard work, filling a vial with the swirly gray concoction. Anna snapped the top on and wrapped it up carefully, and then they flew through the tube to the engine room.

Ravi was waiting outside the *Cloud Cat.* "Where's Niko?" Carly asked as Anna handed Ravi the vial.

Ravi grimaced. "Colin needed him for something, I don't know what."

"That can't be good," Carly muttered.

"Speaking of good," Ravi said, cupping the vial in both hands, "I have good news and bad news. Which would you like to hear first?"

The girls groaned. "The good," Anna replied.

"Well, we figured out how to reconfigure the ship to follow the scent of the dragons."

"Great," Carly said. "So what's the bad news?"

"It will take at least a week to do it."

Their shoulders slumped. Anna scowled.

"What are we going to do?" Carly asked. "All that work for nothing!"

Rocket wandered into the room and lay down at Carly's feet. His ears flopped and she sat on the floor beside him. "I think Rocket's as upset as we are." She began petting his head, hoping it would calm both of them.

Anna stared down at the dog, the wheels turning in her head. "What if . . . ," she said. "What if Rocket could do it?"

"Do what?" Ravi asked.

"Track the scent," Anna replied, tapping Rocket's nose.

"I think we should go get Niko," Carly said, standing up and brushing the dog fur off her leg. "We need to stick together. It's making me nervous that he's not here."

"Okay, let's give Rocket a practice run, then," Anna suggested. "We need something that smells like Niko."

"Hey, ZRKs!" Ravi called out. The two closest ones flew down and buzzed around his head. "Please bring a pair of Niko's socks. The dirtier and smellier the better!"

ZRKs arrived only a minute later, each one clutching a gray

sock in its tiny grip. They dropped them in front of Carly, who picked them up with two fingers and held them as far away from her as possible.

"Okay," she said. "Now what?"

"We need a dog treat," Anna said, pulling a treat from a nearby bag of dog food.

She hid the treat inside one of the socks and stuck out her hand toward Rocket. The dog grabbed for the socks, playfully dropping them and picking them back up. He rubbed his nose in them, frantically coaxing out the treat at the same time. "Good boy!" Anna said encouragingly.

"Poor guy. He probably hasn't eaten since Colin took over," Ravi said.

"Now we have to put a bunch of objects in another room," Anna instructed, "but only one will have a treat on it."

Carly lined up a couch cushion, a foam football, the socks, and one of her own sneakers. "Go find it, Rocket!" Anna said, sending him off to the hall. Rocket sniffed all of them, but picked—not surprisingly—the socks with the treat. Again, Anna made a big deal out of complimenting him.

This time she didn't put out the socks. She led him into the hall and said again, "Okay, Rocket. Go find it." Then she gave him a gentle nudge. She gave the dog one more pat and repeated the command.

Rocket turned in circles, sniffing at the air. Then he ran right at the wall that would lead to the room attached to Chris's. "I think he did it!" Ravi said. "Unless he's just running into the wall."

"Good boy," the girls told Rocket, ruffling him behind the ears.

"All right," Ravi said, "I guess we're heading back down to the lair of the evil twin to see if Niko needs rescuing."

"No need," Niko said, appearing from around the corner. "I've been sprung."

They hurried over and crowded around him. "What happened?" Carly asked. "You okay?"

Niko nodded. "It was weird. He couldn't figure out something in the *Cloud Kitten,* so he made me see if I could get the information out of Chris."

"Chris is awake? That's great!" Carly said.

Niko shook his head. "No, I tried acupressure, but it didn't work. Well, not as well as it does for Dash. He was awake only for a moment—long enough for Colin to ask his question. But I did discover something else."

Carly's face fell. "What is it?"

"Colin said something about there only being one true antidote that would help Chris, which I think means Colin poisoned Chris somehow," Niko said. "He also got nervous when I got near Chris's room, like he was hiding something in there. Maybe there's an antidote?"

"Okay," said Anna, taking charge. "Carly, can you find a way to distract Colin long enough to give Niko a chance to search Chris's room for the antidote?"

"I'm sure STEAM, SUMI, and I can think of something," Carly said with a smile.

"Great. Ravi and I will head to the planet at the same time then and deliver Rocket to the ground crew," Anna said. "That way Colin won't notice us leave the *Cloud Leopard* either."

"But the *Cloud Cat* is linked up to the main system on board," Carly reminded her. "Colin would definitely notice if the *Cloud Cat* leaves."

"We're not taking the *Cloud Cat*," Anna said.

"We're not?" Ravi asked. He sounded a little disappointed. "I'm not sure I'm up for skydiving down to the planet with a dog. Unless the ZRKs have made us flying space-suits?"

The ZRKs buzzed around the room, turning their plastic heads from side to side.

"Nope," Anna said. "We're taking the *Clipper*."

"That piece of junk?" Niko said. "Its propulsion system went off-line, remember? We had to float here."

"I remember," Anna said. "But I also heard Chris say during Gamma that he had the ZRKs repair it. If we're fast enough, and Carly distracts Colin, we can leave without him noticing. As long as our jobs on board get done, maybe he won't figure it out."

Carly nodded. "I think this might work."

23

Dawn on Dargon came fast. One minute, the ground team was sound asleep, with only the glow from their MTBs breaking up the darkness. The next minute, sunlight streamed through the small windows, illuminating the inside of the tank like someone had turned on a thousand-watt bulb. Everyone groaned and flung their arms over their eyes.

The door of the tank banged open. Siena barely had time to swing her legs out of the way. Lythe and Tumar stood framed in the doorway. "Don't you two ever sleep?" Siena groaned.

"A flying ship has landed!" Tumar said, ignoring Siena.

Everyone scrambled to their feet. "Where?" Dash asked.

"Right here," Ravi said. He stood just behind Tumar and Lythe with Rocket at his heels.

"Rocket!" Piper shouted, pushing her blanket aside. The dog bounded into the tank and proceeded to lick her face until she had to push him away. She wrapped her arms around his neck and laid her face on his head. "What's he doing here?" she asked Ravi.

"He's going to find us some dragons!" he replied.

"Huh?" Gabriel asked. "What happened to the original plan?"

"Yeah, the timetable for that wouldn't really work out." Ravi didn't look in Dash's direction.

If Dash noticed, he didn't say anything. He was busy rooting through his backpack. He found his injection needle and turned away from the group to stick it in his leg. When he turned back around, everyone pretended not to notice. "It's okay," he said. "That was my last one. Feels like we should celebrate or something." He gave the group a weak smile, but no one else felt much like smiling.

"So now what?" Gabriel asked, trying to dispel the awkward silence that had fallen.

"Now we get moving." Anna stepped up beside Ravi.

"Where's Niko?" Dash asked, surprised. Anna was supposed to stay on the *Cloud Leopard* to cocaptain with Carly.

"He thinks he may be able to revive Chris," Anna answered. "So I came instead. You'll need me anyway to help with Rocket."

"There they are," Siena said. She had gotten up to search for the ogres. She lowered her binoculars and pointed toward a shady spot on the mountain face. The ogres had gotten higher since yesterday, but were still less than halfway to the top.

Dash sighed. "Okay, we need a new plan, then. Since Chris didn't prepare us to go to the top of the mountain, we're on our own here. We don't even know if there's breathable air up there. If someone should lead Rocket around, it should be me."

"You?" Gabriel asked. "The last person it should be is you, no offense."

"I feel fine," Dash lied. His bones actually ached, but it was nothing he couldn't handle. "The captain is supposed to take the biggest risks, remember? And everyone else has a job. Plus, I need you to go talk to the king."

"I thought I was flying the *Cloud Cat*!" Gabriel complained. He was really hoping to show off his flying skills to Lythe.

"Ravi will have to pilot the ship," Anna explained. "We had to bring the *Clipper* so Colin wouldn't notice us leaving."

Dash nodded. "Besides, Gabriel, you've gotten closer"— Dash cleared his throat and looked at Lythe—"to the elves than anybody else. If anybody can convince the king to hold off on sounding the horn, it's you."

Gabriel smiled and stood a little straighter. "I *am* pretty charming, aren't I?"

Siena kicked him in the shin.

"So," Dash continued, ignoring Gabriel's comment, "Ravi will fly you and Piper with Lythe to meet with the king. We need to know which tree he will allow us to burn so we know which way to steer the dragon. Gabriel, you'll need to radio Ravi with the exact coordinates."

"Roger that!" Gabriel saluted.

"What about me and Anna?" Siena asked.

"You'll go too. Tumar can introduce you to the rest of the elves so you can help them defend their village. If our plan works, we won't need the ogres for anything else and can put them back to sleep as soon as a dragon descends the mountain. But if it doesn't, you'll need to make sure King Urelio doesn't sound the horn too early."

Anna nodded. "Okay, it's a good plan. I say we get started."

24

A nose full of the dragons' scent, Rocket sniffed the air as Dash held on to his collar with a leash he'd fashioned from a vine. Ravi had gone to drop off the rest of the crew at the elves' village and would return to pick up Dash before they startled a dragon out of its lair.

The air on the mountain was thin but breathable. Scattered trees and bushes surrounded deep ravines, and huge boulders hid caves and caverns. There was no evidence of the moss that thrived in the wetter climate below. A good thing, since the rocks were slippery enough already.

The peaks covered so much more space than he ever would have guessed from below. Miles and miles and miles for sure. The view was amazing. The Elfin Forest looked tiny from there. Dash could see the vast ocean and even the land beyond it. Similar mountain peaks grew there, and he wondered if they harbored dragons and ogres too. The silence was total.

He had a brief feeling of being the only person on the planet.

Instead of loneliness, though, a calm settled over him as they walked.

Without Rocket's nose, Dash wouldn't have the slightest idea of where to go. The rocky landscape literally stretched to the distant horizon. Rocket gave one big sniff, then turned south. They came across a long line of wooden huts where the ogres must have once lived. A hundred years of wind and neglect had knocked most of them down, though. The ogres wouldn't be happy to see that, if they made it up there before the horn sounded again.

Soon after crossing a thin stream, Rocket stopped, his paws treading water. Dash almost tipped backward, but Rocket moved forward just enough to pull Dash onto solid ground. "Do you smell something?" he asked. Dash pulled the vial with the synthesized dragon scent out of his pocket. He had Rocket sniff it again, then gave him a dog treat and said, "Rocket, go find it!"

Rocket stepped forward tentatively before picking up the pace. He kept his nose in the air as he went, sniffing passing rocks and tree trunks. Dash lifted his arm and called Ravi. "I think we're getting close," he said into his MTB. "Any word from Gabriel?"

"Not yet," Ravi answered.

"Well, can you call him?" Dash asked, trying to keep up with Rocket, who'd nearly broken into a run. "I think we may have found a dragon!"

Gabriel rushed to silence Ravi's voice, which had suddenly boomed out of Gabriel's MTB while King Urelio spoke.

"Um, I'm talking to him now," Gabriel said, without really hearing what Ravi had asked. His voice sounding strained. "He isn't exactly happy to see us again or to volunteer a tree to burn. And, um, he's kind of glaring at me right now. I guess some of the ogres have been a real pain or whatever."

"Dude, I need the coordinates," Ravi said. "Dash might be face to snout with a dragon right now!"

"I'm doing my best . . . ," Gabriel said.

Rocket led Dash farther up the mountain to an area where land had mostly flattened out. About twenty feet ahead of them, Dash saw part of the rocks move and shift, right next to a huge hole in the ground. He looked closer, thinking the rocks would be part of a dragon, but they were real rocks. The shaking was coming from the dragon below the rocks. The one who may or may not know they were there.

"Good dog," he whispered, slipping Rocket a treat with a shaking hand as Anna told him to.

Instead, Dash found a rock to hide behind at a relatively safe distance (was there really a safe distance from a fire-breathing dragon besides being on another planet?) and crouched down to wait for Ravi.

And he waited.

And then he waited some more.

Dash kept scanning the skies for Ravi and checking his MTB for signs of communication. So far, nothing. He didn't want to make too much noise in case the dragon awoke, but he wasn't sure how long he could wait here either.

He typed off a quick message to Ravi: *Any word yet?*

But Ravi didn't answer.

Come on, Gabriel! Dash thought.

Now his feet were tingling from being crouched down for so long! He decided to call Gabriel.

"Gabe!" Dash whisper-shouted into his MTB, his heart pounding. "I think I'm about to see a dragon. I'd really like to know which way to send it."

"Okay, okay, I got this," Gabriel said.

He listened to Gabriel argue with the king. He should have known the king wouldn't give up one of his trees too easily when the time came.

Gabriel was talking fast. "If you let us burn part of a tree—not even the whole thing—well, okay, the whole thing since we need the roots, but maybe there's one you're tired of looking at? If you do . . . we'll give you the chair you've seen our friend flying in."

"Done!" the king agreed without hesitation.

"Sweet!" Gabriel replied. He'd have to remember to tell Ravi to bring an extra chair down from the *Cloud Leopard.* To Dash, he said, "Easy peasy, dude. I'll get the coords to Ravi."

Dash smiled. "Quick thinking."

"All in a day's work, my friend," Gabriel replied.

After a few moments, the *Clipper* appeared above the rocks and began its descent. No doubt Ravi spotted the creature rising from the hole too. At first, all Dash could see was a row of black horns curving down a scaly spine. That was plenty.

"Meet me on the flat rock formation forty degrees to your left," Ravi instructed, not a minute too soon.

He immediately saw where Ravi meant, but when he tried to go, Rocket wouldn't budge. The dog still wanted to find its target!

"You did it, boy," Dash assured him, petting his back. "But we really don't need to get any closer." It took a few more yanks, but Rocket finally ran alongside Dash toward the ship.

The silence was broken by a sound unlike any Dash had ever heard. It was somewhere between a roar, a scream, a hiss, and static. It was the unmistakable sound of a very angry dragon.

Dash turned around slowly, trying not to attract too much attention. He remembered Chris said the dragons didn't get along with other dragons, and he didn't want to be caught in the middle of a civil war.

A lone dragon had crawled out of the pit. Dash scanned the landscape and didn't see any others stirring, for now. About the size of the transport ship, the beast stood on short, thick legs, its pitch-black eyes fixed right on him. With a shake of its back, two long, scaly wings stretched open. Sharp spikes stood out along the edges. The dragon reared its head at Dash, gnashing two rows of jagged teeth. With nostrils flaring, it breathed a stream of fire right at him. Dash ducked, sheltering Rocket's quivering body with his own. He quickly realized that the flames only extended a few inches away from the dragon's long snout. Either that was all the dragon could do, or it was just getting started. He really didn't want to find out.

Ravi opened the door of the *Clipper.* "Hurry!"

Dash didn't need to be told twice. He pulled a shaking Rocket into his arms and ran to the ship. Every step sent waves of pain up his legs, but he refused to give in to it. The second he closed the door behind them, Ravi took off. The dragon hunched down, then launched itself into the air after them.

25

"Do you know where to go?" Dash asked, breathless. He quickly strapped in.

Ravi nodded, double-checking the coordinates as he lifted away from the mountain. "Here goes nothing," he said, trying his best to outfly a beast that was built to rule the skies. At least they didn't have to worry whether the dragon would actually follow them. That proved to be a resounding yes, yes it would.

Ravi wove through the mountain peaks, ducking and dodging the dragon's fiery breath, before turning down the mountain. He hoped that when Ike Phillips was building the *Clipper* he'd thought to make the ship out of fireproof material. Somehow he doubted it. He glanced over at Dash, who was clutching the arms of his seat as the ship rolled nearly upside down. Rocket whimpered and shivered. Dash pulled the dog close. Ravi wondered who was comforting whom.

He zigzagged his way toward the ground, trying to slow the dragon down by not going in a straight line. Still, he only narrowly avoided the bolts of fire aimed at the back of the *Clipper*. "Listen," he said, glancing at the rear camera as he spoke, "I didn't want to worry you even more by telling you this before, but I don't think Colin's going to give up. There's eight of us and only one of him, but he's super strong. We need to figure out a way to stop him."

Dash yelped as the dragon suddenly sped up and swooped right in front of the ship. One of its huge wings slammed into the front window. A thin crack formed on the surface. The dragon lifted its wing again, and Ravi had to dive far down and bank hard to the left to avoid another attack. He sped up to get in front of it again. He wanted to lead the dragon, not chase it.

"I'll figure out what to do about Colin," Dash promised as Ravi veered out over the ocean before swinging back toward the forest. The dragon stayed hard on their tail.

Dash forced himself to take deep breaths and think. Solving difficult problems was part of what had earned him a spot on the crew and most of what had made him captain. He just needed to focus and consider the situation from all sides, which was basically the last thing he could do in their present situation.

The ship's computer buzzed with an alert. They were in range of the chosen tree. "Look!" Ravi said, pointing out the side window. The elves had drawn a circle around a tree, in what looked like white chalk but probably wasn't. The tree was one of the last ones on the eastern end of the forest, before the forest opened up to the fields of grass and wildflowers.

In front of the tree stood a line of people and elves of various sizes. They could spot at least twenty elves with spears and buckets, Piper and Gabriel (also with buckets), two small, squat figures that Dash knew from the images on the tree must be ogres. There were also giants, one in a dress. A giant-sized pink-and-green dress. Dash blinked and looked again. A strange group of allies if ever there was one. He looked out the back window. The dragon was gone. "Uh, where'd it go?" he asked.

Before Ravi could answer, the ship shuddered and dropped low enough that it was skimming the tops of trees.

"If I had to guess, I'd say it's on top of us," Ravi said as he rolled the ship into a sharp turn. "I'll try to shake him."

Unable to grip the metal with its talons for long, the dragon pushed off, allowing the ship to lift above the trees once more. It started to ascend away from the ship, but not without aiming a massive stream of fire at the ship's nose.

"Now what is it doing?" Dash asked, gripping Rocket's fur tighter.

"He can't get tired yet," Ravi said, deciding their dragon was a boy. "It's almost his big moment." As the dragon looped around to aim another stream of fire at the ship, Ravi made a spiraling turn. "The dragon thinks *we're* the target," he said.

"That's it! Ravi, you're a genius!" Dash cried.

"Uh, yeah, I know," Ravi replied. "How am I a genius again?"

"Does the *Clipper* have a delivery hatch, like for airdropping supplies?"

Ravi nodded. "Sure. It's called 'Open a window and let the ZRKs fly something down to the surface.'"

Dash laughed. "Well, that works too."

"What do you have in mind?" Ravi asked.

"What if we sent down the vial that we used with Rocket? Chris said dragons hate other dragons, so if we put the scent on the tree, maybe our dragon will think another one is near the tree and will fire at it."

"Let's do it," Ravi said. He gave a whistle, and a ZRK pulled away from the ceiling and flew down. Dash dug the vial out of his pocket and placed it in the ZRK's gripper hand. "Be really careful with this," he instructed. "Don't pull out the stopper until you get to the tree. You don't want the dragon to think *you're* the other dragon."

The ZRK gave a short buzz, then waited by the rear hatch. "I'm gonna make this quick," Ravi said. He looped back, aiming toward the tree where the group of elves, humans, giants, and ogres were gathered. Holding his breath, he pressed a button on the control panel. The door slid open just enough to let the ZRK fly out before closing again. Even so, in the second or two it was open, the cabin filled with searing heat from the dragon's breath.

The dragon's head whipped around as he spotted the flying ZRK. With a roar that rattled the *Clipper,* he took off after it.

"Should I follow?" Ravi asked.

Dash shook his head. "You need to get Anna and go back to the *Cloud Leopard,*" Dash said. "I'll have plenty of help here. If Colin realized you left, tell him you were just out testing the new engine. Don't let him know you've communicated with us. I want him to think we still believe we spoke with the real Chris yesterday."

Ravi was curious what Dash was planning, but there wasn't

time to ask. He trusted that whatever it was, it would be brilliant. He set the vehicle down in the field about thirty yards away from the line of assorted creatures, all of them now watching the dragon circling over their heads as it followed the tiny, buzzing round object.

Dash half ran, half dragged himself out the back door. Thirty seconds later, Anna ran in and sat down. "Dash said to wait until you're sure the dragon isn't watching before you go. We don't want him to start following the ship again."

Ravi nodded, placing his hand on the panel, ready to go when the time was right. Their chance came quickly, since the ZRK had just reached the white-ringed tree and dropped its cargo in the branches. The dragon paused, midflight. A loud, wet, snuffling sound filled the air. Then its wings began to beat furiously, and it headed straight toward the tree. The ZRK appeared back on the ship almost instantly, and Ravi took off at top speed.

Dash watched in relief when the dragon didn't even turn around to follow the ship with its eyes. Clearly, once it found new prey, the old one was forgotten. He was surprised that some of the ogres were included in this group of helpers until he saw the spear pointed at them by Tumar and another young elf he hadn't seen before. Everyone ducked as the dragon flew directly overhead, shrieking as it went.

"Where's Siena?" Dash called out to Gabriel. "And Lythe? Are they okay?"

"They're guarding the horn, making sure the king doesn't ring it even when we don't need the ogres anymore!"

Dash glanced away from the tree, which the dragon had begun circling. "Why?"

"Siena thinks that it's cruel and that we don't have the right to do it."

Dash opened his mouth to reply, then closed it again. He couldn't really argue with that. "We can't go back on our promise. The king is living up to his end of the deal; we have to do the same."

"I know," Gabriel said. "But maybe there's a way to get rid of them without, you know, sending them to dreamland forever."

To Dash's surprise, he realized he might actually know a way. But right now he was starting to feel panicked. The dragon's flame hit a clump of leaves on top of the tree, lighting them on fire. The elves let out a group *yelp* like they'd been burned themselves.

Once the first branch ignited, everything seemed to happen in the opposite of slow motion. Dash had hoped that all the moss growing everywhere would have helped keep the fire contained on only the one tree, but that proved not to be the case. The flames sped down the length of the tree, lighting branches on nearby trees as it went. Everyone sprang into action, tossing water from their buckets and kicking dirt on burning leaves. The dragon was still spitting fire, though, making the flames harder to contain. Dash's heart started racing as he pictured all the elves' homes burnt and crumbling. What had they done?

The elves howled in pain as flames continued to spread. Water buckets now empty, the elves directed everyone to fill them with dirt. Dash could barely lift his arms because they ached like he'd just done two hundred push-ups. He coughed, filled his bucket, flung it on burning leaves, coughed, and filled and flung, over and over. His lungs and his arms felt like they were on fire.

Fortunately, he could see Gabriel and Piper working at top speed alongside the elves. They were making quick work of putting out the nearby branches. The fire eventually started to thin out, or nearly out, from all the trees except the one with the circle around it. Everyone had gathered around that one. The top part of the tree was gray now, gnarled and dead. The bottom, still brown and green with bark and moss, was slowly turning purple as the flame reached it. Dash figured the strange color must be from the combination of the heat and chemical makeup of the dragon's fire plus the special wood of the tree. He'd never seen anything like it.

More elves were pouring from the village now, many with ogres marching in front of them, grumbling and stomping. The elves circled the tree, holding hands and swaying. As the flame got closer to the ground, more and more of the tree turned gray and ashen. The parts of the roots that had pushed up through the ground were turning the deep purple of an eggplant.

"Tumar!" Dash shouted to the elf he now considered a friend. "How can I get a message to the king?"

"He's right over there," Tumar said, pointing to the base

of the tree. Dash hadn't noticed the king helping alongside everyone else. His beard was now darkened with ash, and beads of sweat slid down his forehead. Dash ran over to the king and pulled on his sleeve. He had to shout to be heard over all the noise. "King Urelio! I know how to get rid of the ogres so they won't bother you again."

"So do I!" shouted the king. "Sound the horn and make them slumber forever! Take the horn and be gone. That was the agreement, as you well know."

"I know," Dash said. "But it wasn't right for Chris to make that horn, or to promise what he did. I see that now."

The king paused to stare for a second. "You dare to doubt Chrysanthemum?"

Dash would never get used to that name. If the situation wasn't so dire, he probably wouldn't have been able to keep from laughing. But since it *was* dire, he took a breath and said, "Yes. He was alone and desperate to continue his journey, and he wanted to help your ancestors at the same time. We're desperate too, and we also want to help you. But we're not alone. We have options he didn't."

The king looked past him to survey the damage. An elf with white hair began to softly weep. Dash felt awful for being the cause of their pain. Tumar came to stand beside him. "Hey," he whispered. "Don't feel too bad. This tree hadn't been lived in for over four decades. It has root and butt rot."

Dash turned away from the tree to stare at him. He must have heard him wrong. "It has *what*?"

"Root," he repeated, pointing to one of the roots. "Butt."

He pointed to the bottom of the trunk where it met the ground. "Rot."

He'd have been more amused by the funny name if what it implied wasn't so serious. "You're saying the tree is *diseased*?"

Tumar nodded. "I am."

Panic flooded through him. If the dragon cinder came from a diseased tree, would it even work? They couldn't get another dragon here, and the king would never agree to sacrifice another tree. He looked around helplessly, then pointed to the root of one of the trees that sustained burns. "Can we use that one? Maybe we could dig out the root?"

Tumar shook his head. "The root of a living tree will die if exposed to air. If it is dragon cinder you need, you can only get it from a dead tree."

"Do you think it will still work?" he asked.

"I do not know," Tumar admitted.

Dash turned and made his way out of the smoky, suffocating woods. He half sat, half fell to the ground, holding on to the long blades of grass as though they would anchor him to the world. He closed his eyes and took deep breaths. Coughs racked his body, but the air felt cool and fresh now. It would be okay, he told himself. If they got to the ship and the dragon cinder of that tree didn't work, the crew would be able to do it all over again. Somehow they would do it. They just wouldn't do it with him.

He lifted his arm and typed up instructions for SUMI to pass on to the others. Then he called Chris's MTB. As expected, Colin answered, his glasses off. "What is it?" he barked. Then, remembering he was supposed to be Chris, he softened his voice. "Sorry, long day up here. Have you been successful in collecting the dragon cinder?"

As exhausted as he was, Dash forced himself to smile as he would if talking to the real Chris. "It's good to see you, Chris! Yes, we've almost got it! The elves have been very helpful, but they will only give the dragon cinder to you personally. Part of the agreement. I'm sorry for the trouble."

Colin's face twisted into an expression of supreme annoyance. "Fine. I'll be there soon. Then we will load the horn onto the ship as planned and be done with Dargon."

Dash nodded. "Sounds good. I'll send you the coordinates of the meeting place." He typed them in and sent them off.

As soon as Colin's face disappeared, so did Dash's smile. It was replaced by tight-lipped determination.

26

Niko and Carly waited on the other side of the docking bay for Ravi to finish shutting down the *Clipper*. They watched the clock nervously while SUMI hopped around repeating, "I've got the secret plan. I've got the secret plan."

Anna came out first, followed by Ravi. "Is everything okay?" Anna asked first. "Did Colin find out we were gone?"

Niko shook his head. "No, but we have to hurry. He's on his way down here now. Apparently, Dash has a whole plan to get Colin down to the planet and solve the problem of the ogres without putting them to sleep. He sent a message to SUMI with instructions for us. As soon as Colin leaves, we'll explain everything."

"So Chris isn't awake?" Anna asked.

Niko shook his head. "But I think I found the antidote."

"Okay, let's get rid of Colin first," Anna said. "I'll head over to the fuser, but you guys should get out of the engine room now. Spread out across the ship. I don't want him to see us all together and get suspicious."

"How about we meet upstairs in the girls' dorm in five minutes?" Carly said. "Colin would never look there."

They all bumped fists, and Anna went to the fuser. The others swiped three different routes and jumped into the tube. SUMI followed Carly. Colin showed up less than a minute later. He marched over to Anna, who was pretending to check the level of Stinger spores.

"I will be back shortly," he alerted her. "I will have the element with me. I will also retrieve the crew and the horn, so you can tell Ravi he will not be flying down to the planet to get the crew as planned."

Before she could even nod, he stormed off toward the *Cloud Cat*. It occurred to her if he got too close to the *Clipper,* he might see the ZRKs working on the cracked windshield. She held her breath as he paused beside it. He took a step toward it, holding out his hand. Oh no! He must feel the heat coming off it! Then he checked his wrist for the time, scowled, gave the *Clipper* one last glance, and moved on.

As soon as the docking bay doors closed behind them, Anna ran the length of the engine room, calling out for every ZRK in the room to follow her into the tube. They would need all the help they could get.

Anna stood at Chris's usual station on the flight deck and tracked the *Cloud Cat*'s journey to the surface. The small ship showed up as a red dot moving across her screen. When the dot turned blue, she knew the *Cloud Cat* had landed on Dargon. She could tell this landing spot was nowhere near where they'd dropped off the crew. She counted to ten, then hit the emergency shutdown switch.

The dot turned black.

Colin stepped out onto the desolate mountain peak and walked fully around the *Cloud Cat*. All he could see to the east were more mountains. To the west lay a vast ocean and the merest hint of another mountain range on the other side of it. He did not see the ground team, the king, any elves, ogres, or dragons. He especially did not see a sack of dragon cinder.

His hands clenched into fists. He had been tricked. Fuming, he stormed back into the ship. Those horrible children would live to regret this day. He would get the cinder himself, whatever it took. Then he would continue his plan to leave the *Cloud Leopard*—and all its inhabitants—in the cold, dark vastness of space forever.

He sat down, slipped on the flight glasses, put his hand over the control pad, and directed the ship to move.

Nothing happened.

He gave a frustrated groan and tried again.

Again nothing.

No matter how many times he tried, the ship did not move.

After using every troubleshooting trick in the book, Colin realized one thing: this ship wasn't going anywhere.

And neither was he.

Niko had never treated an alien life-form before, and he'd certainly never created a concoction as strange as this. While Carly had managed to distract Colin by helping SUMI and STEAM try to engage (and annoy) the cloned alien in a game of hide-and-seek, Niko had been able to sneak into Chris's room and search for the antidote.

Niko had found notes in Chris's handwriting that described something called Moon Salt, a cure-all for most ailments from the minor to the deadly. There was a detailed description of the chemical makeup of the substance, and although Niko didn't have "the core of a Florian moon pod" (whatever *that* was), he was confident he could re-create the substance.

Now he and Carly rushed to the *Cloud Kitten,* where Chris still lay, passed out.

"And you're sure this will work?" she asked.

"Well, no," Niko answered. "But we don't have any other options at this point."

When they reached Chris, Niko knelt by his side and pulled out a large jar of the replicated Moon Salt.

"Geez, how much of the stuff did you make?" Carly asked.

Niko shrugged. "Enough, I hope." He sat for a moment beside Chris, gazing at his new patient.

"So what do you do now?"

"Well, that's the thing. I'm not sure." Niko scratched his head. Chris's notes only explained what the Moon Salt was, not how it was used.

"Maybe it's like smelling salts," Carly guessed. "You know, to revive someone after they've fainted."

Niko poured out a handful of the salt and held his cupped palm just in front of Chris's nose. He waited. And nothing happened.

"Maybe aliens don't inhale through their nose?" Carly guessed.

Niko brought his palm back, dumping the salt back into the jar. How was this stuff supposed to work?

"Chris," Carly whispered. No response. "Chris!" she said louder, touching his shoulder. "Can you hear us?" A mumble escaped his lips this time but no words. "Chris, come back to us. We almost have the final element!"

Chris's lips began quivering. Niko bent low, putting his ear over Chris's mouth. "Muppet."

Niko looked up at Carly. "Did he say *Muppet*? Like Kermit the Frog kind of Muppet?"

Carly tilted her head at him. "I'm pretty sure aliens don't know Kermit the Frog."

"*Everyone* knows Kermit. That guy's awesome."

"We need to be serious," Carly said.

This time, Chris spoke slower when he responded. "Aaahket."

"Locket?" Niko said.

"Pocket?" Carly replied.

"Which one, do you think?" Niko asked.

"I'm going to guess it's the one he's lying on top of because that would just be our luck."

Sure enough, they had to roll him over, which they did while apologizing the whole time. Carly made Niko reach into the pocket and slip out a thin paper packet. It was filled with something that looked like white Tic Tacs.

"What is it?" Carly asked.

"I don't know," Niko said, taking out a piece and placing it on his palm. It was surprisingly slippery. He tried to keep it from rolling around, but between his cold hands and the lack of friction, it slid right off and landed on Chris's forehead before bouncing off to the floor. Chris's eyes flew open, and he sat bolt upright.

"Whoa," Carly said, flying backward. "Whoa. Was *that* the Moon Salt?"

Chris reached over and threw his arms around her. Carly's eyes opened in surprise. Chris had barely even shaken her hand before. He turned and hugged Niko next, then stood up on shaky legs. "What day is it? Is Dash okay?"

"It's our last day on Dargon," Carly said. "And Dash is okay."

Chris looked past them, toward the open door of the *Cloud Kitten*. "Where is Colin?"

Carly and Niko exchanged looks. Carly took a deep breath. "Well, that's kind of a funny story. . . ."

Dash, Piper, a council of about a hundred official-seeming elves, Lythe, and a smelly group of ogres stood in the field near the burnt tree. Rounding up all the ogres proved to be a lot easier than Dash would have suspected. When the ones the elves had captured saw the tank, they could not stop staring at it and touching it. They literally followed it through the grassy fields like it was the Pied Piper, and they positively drooled. All that steel! All the weapons they could make out of it if it were theirs!

It had been Siena and Piper who guessed that the ogres would be lured by the steel of the tank. While guarding the horn and the sacred tree, they had watched the ogres run through the forest, swinging axes and clanging shields, not seeming to care much if their blades came in contact with anything. They'd treated their axes like their most prized possessions, stopping often to clean them. Siena could see why they were so attached to them. The weapons were incredibly well built, made of metals it must have taken decades to dig up and forge with their primitive technology.

Siena knew firsthand how solid the axes were. She'd borrowed a spear from Lythe and used it like a sword when a group came too close to the Horn Tree. She didn't know if they knew about the horn or what it had done to them, and she didn't want to find out. The elves had never seen sword fighting, so they were very impressed when she single-handedly chased away nine ogres (not counting the one who decided to run just because the others were running). In her air chair, Piper was even more of a celebrity. The ogres fell to their knees when they saw the gleaming metal chair that floated! The elves were so grateful that she'd distracted the ogres from their revenge that there was even some talk of adding her picture to the tree!

Piper turned to Dash. "So you had the idea to use the scent Anna and Carly created to lure the dragon toward the tree, and you came up with a way to get rid of Colin," she said. "You're a smart guy, Dash Conroy."

He smiled at her. "You're not too bad yourself." Piper's cheeks reddened. Fortunately, Gabriel, Siena, Lythe, and Tumai joined them before things got too awkward.

"Well, we've got it," Gabriel said, holding up the sack of dragon cinder.

"Wait . . . the king let you have it?" Dash asked incredulously.

Gabriel shrugged. "You're the one who said I was charming."

Siena rolled her eyes. "Tumar was the one who finally convinced him."

They all looked to Tumar. The elf tilted his head in a sign of respect. "You were as vigilant as some of my fellow elves in protecting our homes. And I explained your new plan to King Urelio. He liked the idea of the ogres being stranded in the mountains on the Wastes of the Misted Isles. Something about the land there being void of precious metals."

Dash didn't know what to say other than "Thank you, Tumar."

Tumar nodded and turned to leave, Lythe following him. They'd only taken a few steps when Lythe stopped. She turned around and lightly stepped up to Gabriel, planting a kiss on his cheek. Then, without a word, she raced back to the rest of the elves, passing Tumar with her dark hair flowing behind her.

Gabriel opened his mouth to say something, but Piper cut him off. "We know, we know," she said. "You're *so* charming."

After contacting the *Clipper,* the group huddled together to wait for Ravi to pick them up. His cheery voice burst through all their MTBs. "*Clipper* to ground team. Landing in one minute."

They looked up to see the *Clipper* streaking toward them. They hadn't seen the *Cloud Cat* go overhead, but those misted isles where Dash had sent Colin were over the horizon from where they stood, so they hadn't expected to. Dash lifted his arm. "Did Colin land? Is he stuck there?"

Anna's voice came across instead. "Yes and yes. Hope you don't mind I came along. I left Carly in charge up there."

Before Dash could tell her it was fine, *Chris's* face came up on their screens.

"Greetings, Voyagers," he said. It was the real Chris! From the echo, Dash could tell Anna and Ravi were hearing it too. "Thanks to your outstanding teamwork abilities, I hear we have a sack of dragon cinder?"

Gabriel held the small bag up. "Yup! It's still warm."

"I do not pretend to understand your resistance to eliminating the ogres once and for all," Chris said, "but I respect your decision and applaud your creativity."

"They still have to agree," Dash pointed out.

"I'm certain they will when they see what you're offering."

The *Clipper* landed. Ravi and Anna climbed out, being sure to close the hatch quickly behind them. Even so, a few ZRKs flew out. The group of ogres gasped and backed away. They hadn't seen a flying machine of this size up close before.

Dash felt strangely heavy as he walked to the front of the crowd, like each leg weighed five hundred pounds. He knew his announcement had to be quick, not only for his sake, but because the elves and ogres traded such angry looks that he knew the situation wouldn't stay civilized for very long. He took a deep breath, then fainted.

27

After a moment of shock, the team leapt into action. Piper took Dash's vitals while Niko dug through his medical pack, looking for anything that might revive their friend. Rocket laid his head on Dash's chest, hoping his buddy would wake up soon. Gabriel secured the dragon cinder onto the ship.

"What can I do?" Ravi asked.

Piper turned and swiped a tear from her cheek as she said, "Dash would insist the mission continue. We have to get these ogres on board along with everybody else."

"All right, I got this." Ravi ran over to the ogres and started grunting and pointing at the ship, motioning for them to board. Captivated by the strange alien who seemed to speak their language, the ogres lowered their weapons and stared at him open-mouthed. Still, they didn't budge.

Siena watched Ravi for a moment while Gabriel, Anna, and Niko carried Dash into the *Clipper,* with Rocket following behind. "Maybe if we drive the tank onto the ship, they'll follow it," Siena suggested to Piper.

"Good call." Piper relayed the idea to Ravi as Siena hopped into the tank. Siena drove while Ravi grunted at the ogres to follow them. They slowly led the ogres into the ship.

Meanwhile, Piper flew to the *Clipper* to help Niko secure Dash. Gabriel hit the navigation controls, and Anna made room on board.

Once everyone and everything was in the ship, Ravi joined Gabriel at the controls.

"Everybody buckle up!" Gabriel shouted. Ravi didn't wait to see if they'd all strapped in before taking off at maximum speed.

Colin sat at the controls of the *Cloud Cat,* pounding out his frustration on the navigation panel. How could he have been deceived by a handful of privileged, snot-nosed children? He slammed his fist down once more and felt the whole ship shake. See? He was smart and strong! How could they not see that he should have been in power of the mission?

But then the ship shook again, and this time Colin hadn't so much as sneezed. Something was pushing on the *Cloud Cat.*

Colin opened an emergency hatch and poked his head out to find a large group of the most hideous and slime-ridden creatures he'd ever laid eyes on. After the initial shock wore off, he saw their potential. *Perfect*, he thought. *Minions.*

Colin cleared his throat. "Hello! I see you like my ship. How would you like to help me make it fly?"

One of the creatures turned to him and grinned. And then it ripped a part of the ship clean off.

Carly raced to the engine room. She wanted to wait to see that Dash was okay but needed to put the dragon cinder into the fuser. As Piper reminded her, the mission came first.

After all this time, the machine was so familiar to her that she could load the dragon cinder with her eyes closed. She didn't, though, of course. She opened the airtight compartment and placed the bag inside, shutting the door firmly. Then she slipped her hands into the slots where built-in gloves would allow her to manipulate the bag without fear of contaminating it. Unlike some of the other elements, there had been no specific amount of cinder necessary. She poured the full bag into the funnel that led to the see-through tubes below. She spent some time calibrating the system, making sure all the levels were equal, before stepping back to judge her work.

The first five slots were completely full now. All that was left to do was to pour in the melted metal from TULIP's belly, which Chris had said should be done at the very last minute so it didn't burn through the machine. They must need a lot of that, because even though there were only six elements, there were seven slots.

At that moment, Gabriel walked in.

"How's Dash?" Carly asked.

"No change," he said. "At least his vital signs are steady."

A very strong, very unfamiliar, very dank and moldy smell wafted from Gabriel's uniform. Carly wrinkled her nose. "What's that smell?"

"That," Gabriel said, wiping his sweaty forehead with the sleeve of his uniform, "is what's left behind when you transport fifty ogres across an ocean."

"Wow," she said, backing up.

"Yeah, it was pretty ripe in there," Gabriel said, "but we got 'em all across. They were happy to go once we offered them the tank. And it was pretty cool dropping the horn to the bottom of the ocean. That thing's probably *still* sinking."

Just when Carly was about to tell Gabriel that she was glad he got back safely (even if he did smell like a herd of ogres), Chris walked in.

"Did you know Colin had been trying to get the *Cloud Kitten* to fly?" Carly asked him.

Chris stiffened. "Oh?" he said.

"We found flight plans. He was going to go back to your home planet! I bet he was going to pretend to be *you*!"

Chris stared straight ahead. His voice was even when he said, "Well, he won't be doing that now."

"Are we really going to leave him there on the mountaintop?" Gabriel asked.

"For now, yes. He'll have plenty of company to boss around now that you've left him a group of ogres to contend with. When we're back in radio range with Earth, I'll send word for someone to rescue him." He paused for a second, then added, "Eventually."

Gabriel and Carly shared a small smile, but it was hard to feel anything but fear and worry when Dash was so sick.

Piper shouted as she soared into the room. "He just said something! I couldn't understand him, but it was something about rotting butts."

"I'm sorry," Chris said, "did you say rotting *butts*?"

Thrilled to have had any progress at all, Piper stifled a giggle. "I'm sure I heard wrong."

"Does rotting butts mean anything to either of you?" Chris asked. Gabriel and Carly shook their heads, also trying not to laugh. It was funny when Piper had said it, but even funnier out of Chris's mouth since he was usually so proper.

Piper led them all to the med bay, where Niko was checking Dash's vitals. Ravi, Anna, and Siena sat in a corner of the room, hopeful expressions on their faces.

Dash's eyelids flickered. His lips quivered, and a whisper came out. "The cinder might not work . . . might be . . . diseased."

Carly took Dash's hand. "Dash, are you okay?" she said, ignoring the possible meaning behind his words.

He wanted to answer her, to tell her he didn't feel any pain, but the effort was too much. He put his energy into moving his head up and down in a nod. It must have worked because Carly loosened her grip a little.

Chris cleared his throat. "I'm going to be really direct here. Dash doesn't have much time, and neither do we." He turned to Carly. "The cinder is in place, I trust?"

She nodded. "All that's left is the liquid metal from TULIP. Is it time to put it in now?"

"Yes. But the metal is so hot I'll be the one taking the risk. Once that is done, I will call you all to the Element Fuser. It will be time to make the Source."

"Rot . . . ," Dash wheezed out. "Fungus."

"Ah, I get it now," Chris said. He rested his hand on Dash's shoulder. "Don't worry. The heat from the dragon's breath will have killed off any fungus."

Dash lifted his hand and attempted to give a thumbs-up.

"Chris," Piper said, "you said you'll need all of us at the fuser, but you don't mean Dash too, right?"

"Everyone," he said firmly. "Listen for my call." He left the room without another word.

"Well," Anna said. "Warm and fuzzy he's not. How are we going to get Dash across the ship? It's not like he can walk, and I'm pretty sure he wouldn't want someone carrying him like a baby."

Siena kicked Anna in the shin, hoping Piper wouldn't notice. Sometimes Anna spoke before she thought.

"He can use one of my extra chairs," Piper said softly.

"I'll go get it from our room," Siena said, hurrying out.

"I'll help," Anna added.

"Me too," Gabriel said, followed by Ravi and Niko.

"Well," Carly said. "That's one way to clear a room!"

Piper laughed. "They should know by now I have a very thick skin. It takes a lot to bother me. In fact, after all the things I've done in this awesome chair, I'm starting to feel like a superhero."

Carly grinned. "You're *totally* a superhero."

The others came back just as Chris called them to the engine room. Niko and Ravi lowered Dash into the chair and tightened the straps so he wouldn't slip out. Piper switched the chair into manual mode, which would allow anyone to use it. Gabriel guided it through the corridor. Rocket followed close behind him.

When they arrived at the Element Fuser, everyone stopped

short. "What's *that*?" Gabriel asked, pointing at what looked like a large, see-through globe with eight bendy tentacle-like arms. A thin glass tube a few feet long ran between it and the Element Fuser.

"Are those Slinkies?" Ravi asked, reaching out a hand to touch one of them.

Chris stepped in front of him. "Please," he said, "don't touch. This is the Source machine, and those are very sensitive hoses."

Gabriel knew machines, and even though he'd obviously never seen a Source machine before, he knew something wasn't right about this one. The arms had clearly been added on once the device was completed. They were made of different material than the base and were of varying lengths. He was about to ask Chris about it when TULIP hopped in front of them and plopped down, head low.

"Poor TULIP," Carly said. "Your belly's all empty. You helped us so much, though. Right, guys?"

Everyone agreed that she'd done a stellar job protecting them from the fate the *Light Blade* had suffered due to their leaky slogger, and keeping them warm down on Tundra. TULIP gave a chirp of appreciation.

Carly glanced over at the Element Fuser, assuming she'd see the last two tubes full of molten metal. Only one had been filled, though. "Did we not have enough?" she asked Chris, pointing to the empty tube. "Or was that one always meant to be an overflow or something?"

Chris faced them and took a deep breath. "I haven't always been honest with you," he began.

His eyes still closed, Dash made a sound in his throat that was halfway between a laugh and a cry.

"And I'm sorry about that," Chris continued. "But it was always for either your own good or the good of the mission."

No one spoke.

"And, well, this is another of those times." He walked over to the fuser. "This empty tube isn't extra. We actually need one more element to make the Source."

Seven jaws dropped open. Dash's would have too if he'd been able to move it. Carly felt a cold sweat break out across her body. "So we're not going home," she said, her voice shaking.

Anna narrowed her eyes at Chris and shook her head.

"What about Dash?" Piper asked quietly.

Siena's eyes stung. She had been quiet since returning to the ship. She'd done something huge down there by taking a stand about not blowing the horn, and didn't think she had any more bravery left inside her.

"Everyone calm down," Chris said, "and let me explain. We have everything we need for the seventh element right here."

"We do?" Siena asked. "Where is it?"

Chris opened his arms wide. "It's inside all of *you*."

28

"**So you harvested** our skin cells without telling us?" Ravi asked after Chris revealed he had brought along their lab samples from the base. "That's kinda shady, don't you think?"

"It wasn't like that," Chris insisted. "We had to make sure everyone was healthy enough to withstand a year in artificial gravity. I knew one of the Source elements came from humans, so it made sense to take the samples when they were no longer needed."

"I don't mind that you took them," Piper said. "But can you just put them in the fuser so we can get on with this?" She glanced worriedly over at Dash. She couldn't tell if he was understanding what was going on or not.

Chris shook his head. "We didn't foresee this, but the cells didn't withstand the jumps to Gamma. They have deteriorated to the point where they will not work at all. I will need to collect new material to go directly into the Source machine." He directed each of them to stand in front of one of the Slinky-like arms and hold one in their right hands. Gabriel set up Dash in front of his and then stood at the next station.

"All you'll need to do, on my count, is hold the tip of the hose against your left palm. You'll feel a fairly strong suction for about ten seconds. I will hold Dash's in place, if that's okay?" He looked to Dash for confirmation.

Dash's head bobbed the slightest bit forward.

The others got ready, putting their hoses into position. Chris pressed a few buttons on a small control panel attached to the bottom of the device. "When the new element is done processing, the elements from the fuser will enter into the round globe you see before you, one at a time. Once they are all inside, they will react with each other on a molecular level, creating the Source. I will then release the tiny amount you need to power the *Cloud Leopard* and deliver you back to your solar system, to the same location we left from."

"You mean, deliver *us* back," Carly said. "To our solar system. Earth's your home now too."

Chris shook his head. "Flora is my home. That's where I'll be going."

They all dropped the hoses in surprise. Dash twitched and made a gurgling sound. "What?" Gabriel said. "You're ditching us?"

"Please don't look at it that way," Chris said.

"So it wasn't Colin who was planning on taking the *Cloud Kitten* to Flora," Carly asked slowly. "It was you?"

He nodded. "I am not certain where Colin was planning to go."

"Are you sure you want to go back to Flora?" Piper asked, putting her hand on Chris's arm. "It's been so long, maybe it won't feel like home anymore."

"For us, a hundred years is not so long," he explained. "Explorers and researchers like myself have traveled even longer than that. No, I must go. But I wouldn't trade my time with you—with any of you—for anything. Each of you has shown incredible bravery, creativity, and skill. Many of you discovered talents you didn't even know you had." He looked at Niko when he said that, and Niko blushed. "You've gone from a group of children to a team of heroes capable of working on your own, and together, for the greater good. Soon your entire world will know it."

Gabriel stepped forward. "It's no secret we weren't so thrilled to meet you when you first showed up. But know I speak for all of us when I say thank you. Thank you for making us feel less alone up here, and for your confidence in us. We'll never forget you."

They took turns giving him hugs and handshakes. Dash managed to put his hand on Chris's, and that was enough.

"Okay, let's do this!" Ravi said. They all picked up the skinny hoses and held them in place. Chris counted down to one, and the suction began. It felt like their whole hand was being squeezed into the tiny opening!

A chorus of "Yowza!" and "Ohhhh!" and a few curses they'd picked up along their journey filled the air. It was all they could do not to yank the hose off their hand. When the ten seconds were up, the suction shut off, and the hoses fell away. They all instantly began rubbing the bright red circle on their palms.

"That was more than a fairly strong suction," Anna said accusingly.

"Really?" Chris said. "I suppose I haven't tried it on actual humans yet. I'm sorry if it was uncomfortable."

"It's okay," Anna mumbled.

"Um, guys?" Siena said, pointing at the round ball in the center of the machine. "Is that our *skin*?" The ball, which had been empty, was now swirling with tiny flakes of all different colors. It looked like confetti.

"Yes," Chris said. "The globe multiplies and magnifies the skin cells a thousandfold. The seventh element requires DNA from nonrelated humans. You eight are ideal because you come from all over the world. That means your DNA will be very different from each other."

"Wait a second," Anna said. "The mission was only supposed to include four humans. If Ike Phillips hadn't sent the rest of us into space and we hadn't joined you at the end, what were you planning to do?"

Chris sighed. "Honestly, I have no idea. I thought I had the DNA I needed. If you hadn't joined us, I would have had to convince you that helping us was your only way home. But if you'd never been sent into space in the first place, well, I guess the rest of us would be living out our lives on Dargon and your planet would soon go dark."

Anna grinned. "So basically what you're saying is that Earth wouldn't have been saved without me and Ravi and Siena and Niko?"

Chris gave a rare smile.

Anna and Ravi high-fived.

The original Alpha crew rolled their eyes. Even Dash groaned.

"If you guys are done congratulating yourselves on sneaking into space," Carly said, "something's happening over there." She pointed to the fuser. The container with the liquid metal had begun to empty out into the tube that led to the globe. With the addition of each new element, the appearance of the mixture totally changed. It went from looking like confetti to a sloshy liquid that coated the inside walls of the globe, to multicolored gum balls with the addition of the zero crystals. The Stinger spores made the balls shatter and form new, smaller ones. The Pollen Slither turned everything silver. Finally, the Rapident powder flew through the tube, turning the Source into a shimmering blue mist. Dash put all his energy into keeping his eyes open to watch. His whole face ached with the effort, but he didn't want to miss anything. This moment was what the whole mission had been about. After a full minute, the shimmering mist didn't change into anything else.

"Um," Gabriel said, looking from Chris to the Source and back. "I'm not sure what I expected, but I kinda thought the Source would look a little, I don't know, *cooler*."

The others murmured in agreement.

"Just wait," Chris said.

Piper began to get antsy. "We don't have time to wait, remem—" But she didn't get to finish. A steady hum filled the room seconds before the top of the glass globe blew open. The swirling mist shot straight into the air. The Voyagers' heads tilted back as the mist reached the high ceiling and fanned out in all directions.

A second later, it rained down on them like tiny snowflakes hitting their upturned faces, their shoulders, their arms. They gasped with surprise, turning to each other in delight.

A shout from Dash made them all turn in his direction. He was standing up from his chair, eyes beaming, grinning from ear to ear. But he wasn't grinning because the Source had given him energy. They followed his gaze across the room, and that's when they saw it.

Piper wasn't in her chair. Piper was *next* to her chair. And she was *dancing*.

"Well," Chris said to himself as the crew whooped and ran across to her, "I didn't see *that* coming."

29

Piper held her arms wide, laughing and weeping as she kicked up her legs, then twirled around in a circle as the mist draped itself around her. She flicked the switch on her chair, and now flashing lights burst through the mist, adding to the otherworldly feel. Dance music blared out of hidden speakers. Dash took Piper's hands, and they moved their legs in a way that was supposed to be dancing but looked more like they were trying to avoid a line of ants. They didn't care.

"How is this happening?" Siena shouted to Chris over the music and the loud hum that still filled the air. They watched as Gabriel took Dash's place, then Carly cut in, and then Dash circled back to dance with them both.

"The Source provides power to energy systems," Chris explained. "The human body is an energy system. And remember, you all are a part of the Source. Your DNA helped create it. That's a very special bond."

Anna ran over. "Are we losing it? That big globe thingy is almost empty!"

Chris shook his head. "The elements need room to combine; that's why the Element Fuser is in the biggest room on the ship. When the globe is empty, the Source will contract and will be sucked back in." He paused. "As long as no one opens the door to outer space. Then we'd be in trouble."

Piper stopped dancing and started running. She ran by them, a streak of blond hair through the mist. The others playfully ran after her. Piper had dreams where she could use her legs again, and she still remembered what it was like before the accident. She didn't want to stop and ask Chris if it would last. She knew it wouldn't. As powerful as the Source clearly was, it hadn't knit her severed spine back together.

Anna nudged Siena and pointed to the globe. The process had begun to reverse itself. The mist was flowing back in, gathering itself up from the floor, from the corners of the room, from their hair and clothes. The hum had gotten noticeably softer too. "We should tell them," Siena said. Anna nodded.

Chris watched as the girls went over to Piper and Dash and put their arms around them and gently guided them back to their chairs. He would miss all of them. He had one last surprise that he thought they'd like, but he would save that for when he took his exit.

When the mist had seeped away from everything except the ceiling, Piper and Dash returned to their chairs. Piper switched off the music and the lights. Dash reached out and took her hand. "I'm sorry," he said.

She knew what he meant, but she shook her head. "It's okay. If I could walk, I wouldn't get to fly." With that, she took off in her chair and hovered by the ceiling until the last drop of mist had fallen back into the Source machine. Chris closed the lid, and the hum abruptly stopped.

Niko stared in awe at the swirling energy that had filled the enormous room and then shrunk to fill a space the size of a beach ball. "What now?" he asked.

"Now we all go home," Chris said.

"Just like that?" Ravi asked.

Chris laughed. "Unless you'd like to travel across another galaxy and collect seven *more* elements first?"

Ravi put up his hand. "No thanks, dude. I'm good."

"You all go up to the navigation deck," Chris instructed. "I'll take care of getting the Source into the system, and I'll meet you up there."

He watched them go and then got to work.

The ZRKs had brought everyone's favorite snacks from the storerooms and spread it out on tables. Everyone dug in like they hadn't eaten in a week. Dash was able to move his hand to his mouth, and Carly held his cup steady to his lips. Piper was quiet, lost in her own thoughts.

Monitors all around the room lit up, and everyone stopped chewing to look. Chris's face appeared on the screens. At first, they couldn't tell where he was, but then realized he was inside the *Cloud Kitten,* and the *Cloud Kitten* was in space!

"I guess you're not big on long good-byes!" Carly said.

Chris smiled. "I thought it was best this way. I'm going to wait here and make sure the Source works before heading to Flora. And there's one more thing. . . ."

The door to the navigation deck slid open. Rocket came bounding in, a new bell around his collar.

"Rocket!" Piper called out, zooming over to him. She bent over to put her arms around the dog's neck. Over her shoulder, she asked, "You didn't take him with you?"

"He's an Earth dog," Chris said. "He belongs to all of you now. I thought you could take turns."

"When it's my turn," Gabriel said, "I'm going to take that embarrassing bell right off him."

"It's not a bell," Chris said. "It's a small container with a video chip in it. I'd like you to give it to Shawn when you get home. We never got to say a real good-bye." His voice cracked a little. "He was an excellent friend to me. I hope I was good to him too."

"You were for sure," Carly said. "We could all see it."

His eyes got glassy for a second, then focused again. "Thank you. Travel swift and safe."

"Will we see you again?" Piper asked.

Chris winked. "Not if I see you first."

Everyone laughed. "*Now* he gets a sense of humor!" Gabriel said.

"C'mon, guys," Anna said. "It's time to go home. Dash doesn't look so good. *Again!*"

Everyone hurried to strap themselves in. Anna took the

seat Chris usually sat in. It was understood that she'd be the one pressing the button this time.

"Is this going to hurt?" Gabriel asked, only half kidding.

"You won't feel much of anything," Chris assured them.

"That's what you said about the Source machine," Anna muttered.

"Everyone ready?" Chris asked, looking around the room.

For such a simple question, it caught all of them off guard. Were they ready to cover the same distance in a second as it took a year to travel at Gamma Speed? No. Were they ready to deal with the fame and attention that would await them at home? Not really. Were they ready to leave each other? Definitely not.

But they were ready to see their families and friends from home. They were ready to put their feet on solid ground and keep them there. And most of all, they were ready to hand over the Source.

Dash tried to reply, to give his last command as captain, but his throat wouldn't work.

Anna looked at Dash, then at everyone. "We're ready," she said.

"Then hit the red button," Chris said. He faced Dash and gave him a salute. Dash raised a shaky arm and saluted back.

Anna hit the button.

30

Before Gabriel could finish saying "Whoa, that feels weird," the blue oceans of Earth appeared in the lookout window. The Voyagers' mouths fell open in surprise.

"Is that real?" Siena asked, hardly breathing. "Are we home?"

"I . . . I think so," Carly managed.

"We are inside Earth's atmosphere," Ravi announced. He unlocked his harness, and the others followed.

"Man, that Source is powerful stuff!" Niko said, shaking his head.

Dash took a deep breath, then another. He couldn't believe he was there. He couldn't believe he was alive at all. Gratitude washed over him in waves.

Piper sped over with Rocket barking behind her. "Dash, how do you feel?"

"I'm good. I'm really, really good!" He gulped in deep breaths and licked his dry lips. "Thank you for taking such good care of me all year."

"That's my job," she said, smiling. "Thank you for dancing with me."

The others had started jumping up and down, laughing, high-fiving. Piper and Dash watched them, and then Dash grinned back at her. "All in a day's work," he replied.

The long screen above the wraparound window flickered, and Commander Phillips's face appeared, tears flowing freely down his cheeks.

"You're . . . you're all . . . I can't . . . and Dash, you're . . ."

"All right, all right, you had your chance," a little girl's voice said, pushing Phillips out of their view. Dash saw his sister Abby's face and lit up. She looked older than in the last video he'd received months ago, but she was definitely the same spunky girl.

"Dash! Are you okay? How was it? Did you meet any more aliens? Did you guys save the world? Did you bring me anything? Do you have a girlfriend now?"

Dash laughed. "No girlfriend, but Gabriel did get kissed by an elf."

Carly gave Gabriel a puzzled look, but all Gabriel did was grin.

Commander Phillips came back on the screen.

"Are our families there too?" Carly asked, trying to peer over the commander's shoulders.

He shook his head. "Since we lost communication, we didn't know exactly when you'd be back. Because of Dash's condition, his mother and sister came to live on the base. We will be flying in everyone else tonight—including your families, Anna, Siena,

Ravi, and Niko. You were instrumental in creating the Source, so you'll also receive the prize money promised to the Alpha Team."

The Omegas erupted into cheers.

"The crew here will connect with the ship's computer remotely now and will navigate the *Cloud Leopard* back to base," Commander Phillips continued. "Once you're back, we'll initiate decontamination mode, which means the air coming through the vents in the ship will be specially treated to destroy any pathogens or microbes you might have picked up on your journey."

"So what you're saying," Ravi said, "is that it wouldn't do much good if we saved the world and then killed off every living creature because of some strange disease we picked up on the other side of the galaxy?"

"Well," Phillips said, "I wouldn't have put it quite that way, but yes."

"Okay, cool, just making sure."

"It won't take long," he promised. "By morning, you will be ready to face the world. Do you think you guys can stand being on board together for one more night?"

They all exchanged looks. Gabriel glanced over at the table full of desserts the ZRKs had set out. "There's still some popcorn left," he said to the others. "You guys thinking what I'm thinking?"

"Movie night!" they shouted.

The ZRKs had made them brand-new uniforms for their homecoming. Silver instead of blue, they still had the holographic *V* on the chest for *Voyagers,* but around the *V* were symbols for each of the seven elements. For the seventh element, the ZRKs had made a new symbol—it was an *O* for *Omega* entwined with an *A* for *Alpha*. Carly had told them what Chris had said, about them being a part of the Source now. The uniforms would remind them of that every time they looked at them. Not that they'd forget it, or anything that had happened—even the parts they might like to!

After getting dressed in the new uniforms and packing what little they had brought with them (and the souvenirs they'd collected along the way), the whole team had planned to meet in the cargo docking bay, where they'd disembark the *Cloud Leopard* for the last time. Carly and Gabriel were the first to be ready, and they waited in the docking bay for the others.

They smiled awkwardly at each other. After living together for a year, it was hard to believe it was time to say good-bye. Usually, they'd have plenty to say to each other, but now it was hard to find the right words. Carly thought back to the first night she'd spent with Gabriel back at Base Ten, the night they'd discovered that Shawn had been hiding the truth behind the mission. She couldn't start reminiscing already.

"So," Carly said, "you kissed an elf?"

Gabriel grinned, leaning back with his arms behind his head. "What happens on Dargon stays on Dargon!"

Carly laughed and shoved him playfully.

Niko and Siena wandered in next, followed by Ravi, STEAM, and SUMI. Siena was showing Niko the photos of the dragon on her arm tech.

"These shots are amazing. Siena, I could kiss you!" Niko exclaimed.

"Um, please don't," Siena said, leaning back. "How about I just send them to your MTB?"

Niko smiled. "Perfect."

"What are you guys going to do with the money?" Ravi asked.

"I hope they give it to us all in one-dollar bills," Gabriel said.

"Why?" Siena asked.

"So I can make it rain!" Gabriel held up both hands and mimed tossing money into the air. Everyone laughed.

When Anna strolled in, she carried more luggage than any of them. Most of the Voyagers had one small duffel bag filled with personal belongings. Anna had three.

"What?" she said. When the rest of the crew continued to give her blank stares, she said, "ZRKs don't need twenty bottles of lavender-scented shampoo. I just don't want it to go to waste."

Just then, Anna's MTB started to buzz. She looked down at the screen and shook her head. "Sorry, Ike Phillips. I don't know how you got this frequency, but you're silenced forever." She hit the ignore button on her wrist and smiled at Carly.

Carly smiled back and gave her a high five. "Where are Piper and Gabriel?" she asked.

"We're here!" Piper called. She glided slowly next to Dash, who carried her duffel for her. "It's good to be home." Piper's smile stretched so wide the others could see her dimples from across the room.

"I think we're all feeling much better now that we're back home," Ravi said.

"Yeah, but I'm going to miss you guys," Carly said.

Gabriel threw his arm around her shoulders. "Me too."

"Definitely," chimed in Niko.

Ravi and Siena nodded. Piper took Dash's hand.

Then they all looked at Anna.

"Don't look at me, I can't wait to get away from all of you," she said. Then she grinned. "Just kidding. You guys ended up all right in the end."

"Ladies and gentlemen, I think Anna Turner just said she likes us," Ravi announced.

They all laughed. Even Anna.

"You sure they'll let us keep the Mobile Tech Bands?" Siena asked.

"My dad always says, *If you don't ask, they can't tell you no*," Anna said.

They all laughed. Dash knew they would be allowed to keep them if they asked, but it was fun to pretend like they were being sneaky. After all, they hadn't felt like kids in a long time. So he said, "Okay, but I'm pretty sure right now they'd let us keep the *Cloud Leopard* if we asked!"

"That reminds me!" Gabriel said. He looked up at the ceiling and whistled. Two ZRKs flew down and landed on his shoulders.

"Seriously?" Piper asked.

Gabriel pretended to pout. "Hey, you're keeping your air chair! I should get something too."

Piper grinned. "Fair enough."

A communication screen on the wall flickered to life, and Shawn's face appeared once more.

"Good morning, Voyagers," he said.

"Good morning," they replied.

"If I asked to keep the *Cloud Leopard*," Gabriel said, "would you say yes?"

Commander Phillips laughed. "No."

Gabriel nodded. "Just wondering."

"But you can keep the MTBs," he said with a wink.

"If you insist," Piper said, trying to look innocent.

"Well," Shawn said, "are you ready to come back home?"

They all looked at each other. This was the moment they'd all been waiting for. Their mission was over. Now their futures lay before them. Were they ready?

Dash cleared his throat. "Let's get those lights turned back on, Commander Phillips."

Shawn smiled. "All right, I'm going to have the base crew open the docking bay doors, then. See you in a few." The screen went black, and everyone held their breath, waiting for the moment the doors would open and they could finally step foot back on their home planet.

"So this is it," said Dash. He looked at Carly, his second-in-command and the best first mate a captain could ask for. He looked at Gabriel and wondered if he'd ever meet anyone as funny and talented. And then he looked at Piper. Piper squeezed his hand.

"I think we're ready for it," she said. She reached out and took Gabriel's hand. Gabriel smiled and took Carly's hand.

With smiles a mile wide, the eight Voyagers stepped up to the docking bay doors. Their families were waiting outside for them, along with reporters from hundreds of news stations. Giant screens would beam the homecoming live to televisions and computers all over the world.

A rumble sounded, and they weren't sure if it was the sound of the doors opening or the audience of thousands as they shouted and clapped. Light from the Earth's sun flooded in, warming the Voyagers' faces for the first time in over a year. They were home.

Wendy Mass is the *New York Times* bestselling author of *The Candymakers* and nineteen other novels for young readers, including *A Mango-Shaped Space, Jeremy Fink and the Meaning of Life* (which was made into a feature film), *Every Soul a Star,* and the Willow Falls series, which began with *11 Birthdays.* Her latest is *Pi in the Sky* and a new series for beginning readers called Space Taxi. She is currently finishing up the sequel to *The Candymakers* while building a labyrinth in her backyard. Not at the same time, of course. That would be weird. Visit her at wendymass.com, where she'll tell you that while writing Voyagers #6, she discovered that she'd waited far too long to write a book featuring elves and dragons, because what's more fun than that?

READY TO JOIN TEAM ALPHA?

Download the Voyagers Game App!

► Test your knowledge about science and space

► Repair your ship

► Steer your ship through Gamma speed

► Explore new planets

► Build ZRKS

► And check out bonus content with every new book!

The *Cloud Leopard* **will** return to Earth.

THE ADVENTURE DOESN'T END HERE.
UNLOCK ALL THE MYSTERIES AT VOYAGERSHQ.COM

- PLAY SPACE-AGE GAMES
- CUSTOMIZE YOUR ZRK COMMANDER
- EXPLORE THE VOYAGERS UNIVERSE
- AND MORE!